OWL IN THE OFFICE

"This could be the last creature I'm able to help, I'm afraid, Mandy. The buildings are badly in need of repair and it's going to cost at least five hundred pounds to have them done."

"Five hundred pounds!" Mandy gasped.

"Yes," Betty said, shaking her head. "And to top it all, Sam Western's raised my rent. I simply don't have enough money to pay him, do the repairs, *and* feed the animals as well."

"But you *can't* close down, Betty," Mandy said, almost in tears. "You just can't! What will happen to all the animals you've got here?"

"I'll find homes for as many as possible," Betty said. "But I'm afraid the rest will have to be destroyed."

Give someone you love a home!
Read about the animals of Animal Ark™

OWL in the OFFICE

Ben M. Baglio

Illustrations by Shelagh McNicholas

**Cover illustration by
Peter Mueller**

AN
APPLE
PAPERBACK

SCHOLASTIC INC.
New York Toronto London Auckland Sydney
Mexico City New Delhi Hong Kong

To Rats and Jess and their cousins,
Midge and Milo

Special thanks to Sue Welford for all her help.
Thanks also to C. J. Hall, B.Vet.Med., M.R.C.V.S.,
for reviewing the veterinary information contained in this book,
and to Tom Tyrell of the Tomar Owl Sanctuary.

No part of this publication may be reproduced in whole or in part, or stored in a retrieval system, or transmitted in any form or by any means, electronic, mechanical, photocopying, recording, or otherwise, without written permission of the publisher. For information regarding permission, write to Working Partners Limited, 11A Dunraven Road, London W12 7QY, United Kingdom.

ISBN 0-439-08416-4

12 11 10 9 8 7 6 5 4 3 2   9/9 0 1 2 3 4/0

Printed in the U.S.A.   40
First Scholastic printing, July 1999

One

"Quick, James — over here!" Mandy Hope shouted to her friend James Hunter. She knelt down in a pile of last autumn's fallen leaves, gently brushing some aside.

Mandy and James were out walking in Monkton Woods near Welford, the Yorkshire village where they lived. Mandy had spotted something in the carpet of leaves beneath one of the oak trees.

"What have you found?" James ran over and skidded to a halt beside her. His sneakers sent up a spray of leaves. He pushed his glasses back up his nose and looked down at the little hollow Mandy had made in the leaves.

Mandy cupped her hands together and lifted something very carefully from the ground. She held what looked like a bundle of bedraggled feathers. Two round, dark eyes stared at James. A sharp, hooked beak opened and a kind of creaky noise came out. It sounded like a gate that needed oiling. Mandy drew in her breath. She gazed up at James with shining eyes.

"Oh, look! It's a baby owl."

James touched the tiny creature gently with his fingertip. "What kind of owl is it?"

"A tawny owl, I think," said Mandy. "Oh, the poor thing!" She had thought it might be an owl when she first spied the bundle of gray-brown flecked feathers lying in its hollow of leaves. Although she'd seen pictures of baby owls she had never actually seen a live one. It felt soft and beautiful and very fragile.

"Wow!" exclaimed James. His eyes were round behind his glasses. "Where did it come from, Mandy?"

Mandy looked up into the huge oak tree, its great branches reaching up to the sky.

"Up there somewhere," she said, frowning. "You can never really see owls' nests; they're too well hidden. It's probably where two of those big branches meet or maybe in an old squirrel's nest somewhere."

Mandy's heart jolted with pity. "Poor thing," she murmured again.

James squinted upward, pushing back the peak of his baseball cap to get a better view. "Maybe we could climb up and put it back in its nest," he suggested hopefully.

Mandy knew it would be the best solution. The owl wouldn't survive for long out in the open, that was for sure. But how on earth were they to reach it?

"We'd need a ladder." Mandy tucked a strand of blonde hair behind her ear. Her brows knitted together over her blue eyes in a thoughtful frown. "Or maybe I could climb up?" she said, not sounding at all sure. She had long legs and was pretty good at climbing trees, but this one had a tall, straight trunk with no footholds at all.

"No way," said James with a shake of his head. "The first branch is miles up. Don't you think we should just leave it where it is?"

Mandy stared at him in horror. "We can't do that! It'll get eaten by a fox or something!"

James shrugged. "I read somewhere you should leave baby birds alone. Sometimes their parents come down to feed them."

Mandy shook her head. "Owls mostly come out at night," she said. "It could be too late by the time they find him." She heaved a sigh. There was only one thing to do then. They would have to take the baby owl back to Animal Ark. Her mom and dad were both veterinari-ans. They would know what to do.

"We'll have to take him back with us," she said to James.

James bit his lip. Once Mandy made up her mind about something, there was no changing it.

James whistled to his dog. Blackie crashed through the undergrowth toward them.

"Come on, Blackie." James patted the Labrador's sleek head. "Time to go home."

But Blackie was too interested in Mandy's mysteri-ous bundle to take any notice of his master. He jumped up, sniffing the owl's feathers.

"Down," Mandy commanded. Blackie ignored her and went on sniffing.

James pulled the dog's collar gently. "Blackie, do as you're told!"

Blackie wasn't the most obedient dog, but this time he listened to James and allowed himself to be pulled away from the baby owl.

Mandy carefully wrapped the owlet in her scarf and cradled it gently in her arms. "Come on, James. The sooner we get this little thing to where it's warm, the better."

Blackie soon lost interest and trotted on ahead.

"What do you feed owls?" James trudged along by

Mandy's side as they made their way through the woods out toward the road that led to the village of Welford.

Drs. Emily and Adam Hope ran a busy veterinary practice in the village. They had adopted Mandy when she was a baby. Her birth parents had been killed in a car crash and Mandy couldn't remember anything about them. The Hopes were the only parents Mandy had ever known. As far as she was concerned, nobody could wish for a better mother or father.

James, a year younger, was Mandy's best friend. He shared her love of animals. Mandy and James both went to school in the neighboring town of Walton. Today, though, was the first day of their spring break.

"I'm not sure," Mandy said in answer to James's question. She knew that in the wild, owls hunted for small mammals like mice and voles. Owls hunted mostly at night, although sometimes you saw them out in the daytime, especially during springtime when they had young to feed. But Mandy couldn't exactly imagine catching little furry animals to feed the baby owl. In fact, Mandy wasn't sure *what* she was going to do with it. All she knew was that they couldn't leave the tiny, helpless creature out in the woods with no one to protect it.

The bird peeped out with huge, scared eyes as they made their way across the village green toward the old stone cottage with its wooden sign that said ANIMAL ARK

VETERINARY CLINIC. Dr. Emily and Dr. Adam had started the practice when they got married. Dr. Adam had lived in Welford all his life, and both he and his wife were well known and popular members of the village community.

Mandy and James hurried in through the clinic door. Jean Knox, the receptionist, was busy at her computer. She looked up as Mandy and James burst in.

"Where are Mom and Dad?" Mandy asked breathlessly, cradling the owlet against her coat.

Jean glanced at the appointment book in front of her. "Your dad's gone up to Syke Farm and your mom's indoors." She peered over the top of her glasses. "What *have* you got there, Mandy?"

Mandy went closer and gently peeled back the woolly scarf.

Jean's hand flew to her mouth. "Oh, my goodness. Where did you get that?"

Mandy explained quickly.

"We couldn't possibly reach the owl's nest," James blurted. "So we had to bring it here."

"Well, what will you do next? Take it out to Simon. He'll know what to do," Jean said matter-of-factly. It was no real surprise to her when Mandy arrived home with a sick or abandoned animal. If Mandy had arrived home with a baby elephant, Jean probably wouldn't have batted an eyelid. Mandy loved all animals and wanted to be a vet herself one day.

Simon, the veterinary nurse, was sterilizing the surgical instruments. It had been a busy morning: a cat with a thorn in its paw; a dog that had swallowed a sock; five puppies for injections; a rabbit with pneumonia; and a gerbil whose babies were ready to be born. Then, to top it all, fussy Mrs. Ponsonby from Bleakfell Hall had arrived with Pandora, her pampered Pekingese, just as they were closing. It had taken all of Dr. Emily's powers of persuasion to convince Mrs. Ponsonby that her dog didn't have the flu, just a runny nose.

Simon looked up and grinned when Mandy and James walked in.

"Hello, you two," he said cheerily. "What have you been up to this morning?"

"We found this . . ." Mandy pulled back the scarf to reveal the baby owl.

"Oh, wow!" Simon touched the creature's head. "Where?"

James explained.

Simon frowned and ran his hand through his fair hair. "You know, you should really have left him there."

"I *told* you!" James said.

Mandy began to wonder if she had done the right thing in bringing the owl to the clinic. But it was too late now. Rightly or wrongly she had brought him home and it was now her responsibility to look after him. "But I couldn't just leave him," she protested.

Simon pulled a wry face. "I know it's hard, Mandy, but the parents may have come down to feed him — or he might have been able to find his way back to the nest."

Mandy shook her head firmly. "No, I'm sure he's too weak for that."

Simon looked at the tiny creature. "Well, maybe you're right. If he's the smallest chick, the others probably hogged all the food and he probably would have starved to death anyway."

Simon pulled back the scarf a little more. "He's very tiny. I'm afraid it's the survival of the fittest where birds in the nest are concerned. Nature can be very cruel at times."

"It certainly can," Mandy said. The little owl looked so sweet. To never have known if he lived or died would have been too much to bear.

"I think the best thing to do . . ." Simon suggested, "is to take the little fellow up to the animal sanctuary. I'm sure Betty Hilder will know what's best."

Just then, Emily Hope came through the door. She was still wearing her white vet's coat, and her red hair was tied up with a green silk scarf. She smiled. "Hi, you two." Then she spied the small bundle in the crook of Mandy's arm. "What have you brought us now, Mandy?"

Mandy quickly explained.

"Simon says we should have left him there," said James.

Dr. Emily raised her eyebrows. "Yes, you should have, really. But since now he *is* here, let's take a look at him."

"Simon suggested we take him up to Betty," said Mandy.

Dr. Emily agreed. "Good idea," she said. "I'll take a look at him first, though. He could be injured. Was he just lying on the ground?"

"Well, he was *sitting* on the ground," Mandy said. "In fact," she added, "I almost stepped on him."

"OK," Dr. Emily said in her usual businesslike manner. She took a pair of surgical gloves out of their sealed plastic package and pulled them on. "Sit up on the examining table, Mandy, and I'll take a look at him."

Mandy heaved herself up. She gently unwrapped the little owl and set him carefully on her knee. Free of the woolly scarf, he shook his feathers, staggered, and almost fell. His sharp claws gripped the knee of Mandy's jeans as he struggled to regain his balance.

Mandy put her hands on either side of the owl to

steady him, smoothing down the soft feathers. She was surprised to feel how tiny his body was. The owl sat there blinking in the bright overhead light. Then, without warning, he flapped his wings and tried to fly, overbalancing completely and landing in a heap on the scrubbed tiles of the clinic floor.

Mandy jumped down and bent to retrieve him, worried that the owl had landed awkwardly. It would be too bad if the little bird had survived his fall from the nest, then ended up hurting himself on the clinic floor!

"Watch those talons," her mother warned. "You might get a nasty scratch."

Mandy put her hands on either side of the bird's wings. "Now, behave yourself, Mr. Owl," she said sternly. The owl blinked at her and made a squeak. Mandy couldn't help smiling. He looked rather indignant at being handled by a human being! She set him down on her knee again. This time, he stayed where he was.

Dr. Emily quickly examined the bird. Feet, wings, fluffy head. Finally she smoothed down his feathers. "He's very thin," she said, frowning. "Skin and bone. I reckon he hasn't been getting much food. Just wrap him up again, Mandy. I'll take a look at his eyes and beak."

"Mom, can't I keep him here?" Mandy said. "I'll look

after him, I promise. I'll get food for him and everything."

Dr. Emily shook her head. "Sorry, Mandy. Looking after baby owls is really very specialized. Simon's right — we'd better take him to the sanctuary. Betty will know what's best."

Mandy knew better than to argue with her mother. A veterinary clinic was no place to keep a baby owl. However much Mandy longed to take care of him, she knew expert help was needed.

Dr. Emily looked at her watch. "I could take you up there now if you like. I haven't got any calls to make until later."

"That would be great, Mom. Thanks." Mandy got down off the couch. "Coming, James?"

"You bet!"

"You'd better put Blackie in the back," Dr. Emily told James when they got outside. Blackie was still trying to find out what Mandy had in her arms, jumping up and sniffing at the scarf. "He seems a little too nosy if you ask me."

Blackie was always curious about everything. And his curiosity often got him into trouble.

James opened the rear door of the four-wheel drive and banged his hand on the floor. Blackie jumped inside.

"Stay!" James commanded.

For once, Blackie did as he was told. He sat looking out of the window, his tail wagging like mad. Every trip in a car was an adventure to him.

They all piled in and Dr. Emily set off through the village. She turned off past the post office, heading for the narrow hilly road that led up to the Welford Animal Sanctuary.

"Mom," Mandy said when they were halfway there. She had been feeling upset about taking the owl away from his natural environment. "I'm sorry if I've done the wrong thing."

Dr. Emily patted her knee. "It just might be better to ask someone's advice next time, that's all."

"I will," Mandy promised. She made a vow to listen to James more, too. She couldn't *always* be right.

Mandy had been to the sanctuary several times before and knew its owner, Betty Hilder, very well. Although she loved seeing the animals Betty had rescued, her heart always went out to them. She knew that most of them would have had to be put to sleep if Betty hadn't taken them in. There were creatures of every kind. Dogs, cats, donkeys, a Shetland pony, an ancient goat with three legs. The last time Mandy had been there, Betty even had a Vietnamese potbellied pig that someone had brought in.

"They had bought it as a pet," Betty had explained to Mandy. "No one ever told them that pigs are extremely difficult to house-train."

The car crested the summit of the hill and began the winding descent down the other side.

Mandy gazed out of the car window at the panorama of hills and dales. The drystone walls made a picturesque pattern across the landscape. The sky was blue and broad, not a cloud to be seen.

Mandy loved it up here on the moor, the village of

Welford spread out below. There were the two roads, the church and the village green in the middle. A pall of smoke rose from the row of quaint old cottages behind the Fox and Goose pub. Her grandpa's friend Walter Pickard lived in one. They'd both been bell ringers at the church for years. Mr. Pickard must be having a bonfire, probably burning his garden clippings. The village people took great pride in their gardens, and Walter grew roses that won prizes at the Welford County Fair every year.

Dr. Emily changed gear and swung the four-wheel drive around into the drive that led up to the sanctuary. To Mandy's dismay, the gate was shut and locked.

"Oh!" she exclaimed, puzzled. "I've never seen it shut before."

Mandy wondered what on earth had happened. Betty was always proud to be able to say the sanctuary was open any time.

Dr. Emily pulled up in front of the gate. "Maybe she's gone out shopping," she suggested. "I'll just get out and see."

Dr. Emily went up to the gate. She stood frowning at the rows of kennels and outbuildings that housed the rescued animals. Then, Betty Hilder, a young woman dressed in baggy jeans and a thick sweater, came out of her bungalow and hurried to open the gate. She spoke to Dr. Emily.

"I wonder what they're talking about," said James.

"I don't know," said Mandy, still worried. "Betty looks pretty upset."

Betty took out a key and unlocked the gate. Dr. Emily came back to the car looking grim. As soon as she opened the door they bombarded her with questions.

"What's up, Mom?" asked Mandy, her heart pounding. She had a feeling something really serious was going on.

"Why is Betty looking so upset?" asked James.

Dr. Emily turned on the ignition. "I'm afraid it's bad news, you two," she said. "Betty's letting *us* in, but she's had to close the sanctuary to the general public."

Mandy leaned forward anxiously. "Closed! Mom ... why?"

Dr. Emily drove through the gate and into the concrete yard. A chorus of dogs greeted the newcomers as they got out of the car. In the back, Blackie barked excitedly and clawed at the window.

"Quiet, Blackie!" James commanded.

"Betty's very short of money," Dr. Emily told Mandy and James as she shut the car door. "She just can't afford to keep things going."

"What will happen to the animals?" said Mandy. She glanced down at the tiny, helpless bundle in her arms. If Betty wasn't going to be able to look after the baby owl, then who would? There wasn't another sanctuary for miles.

Her mother glanced at her. "If homes can't be found, then —" She broke off. Mandy had a horrible sinking feeling she knew exactly what her mom was going to say. If homes couldn't be found for the animals, then they would all have to be destroyed!

"No!" Mandy turned to James. "We can't let the animals be put to sleep," she cried. "We've got to do something. We've just *got* to!"

Two

As Mandy went toward the bungalow, clutching her precious bundle, Betty pulled back the scarf and took a peek at the owl.

"Poor thing," she said. "Bring him into the office, Mandy. It's warmer in there."

They went into the room where Betty kept her old typewriter and telephone. There were papers all over the desk, photos of cats and dogs on the wall, and a bucket of pony treats in one corner.

Two cats came over and rubbed themselves against Mandy's legs. Betty shooed them out. She went through another door and brought back a large cage with a wooden back. "We'll put him in this hospital cage for the time being," she said. "He's got to be isolated in case he's carrying any pests or diseases."

Mandy handed over her precious bundle. Betty quickly examined the bird.

"I've already taken a look at him," Dr. Emily confirmed. "He's uninjured but very thin. I think he must have been the smallest of the brood."

Betty went over to the cupboard and took out a plastic bottle. She covered the owl's face with one hand, then quickly puffed a white powder into his feathers.

"That's to get rid of any vermin," she explained.

Betty placed the owlet carefully in the cage. A cloud of white dust flew out as he shook his feathers, then settled in one corner looking hunched up and miserable.

Betty perched on the edge of the desk. She looked thoughtful. "I've had a couple of owls before," she said. "They both went over to Longmoor Owl Rehabilitation Center. Once I've persuaded this one to eat properly I'll take him over there. They'll keep him for a few weeks, then release him back into the wild as soon as he's fit."

"Couldn't we do that?" asked Mandy. She felt disappointed. She would love to have seen the owl fly safely away.

Betty shook her head. "I'm not licensed to do that,"

she explained. "And the owl must never be handled again once he's accepting food, otherwise he'll never be able to be released. I haven't got those kinds of facilities here, Mandy."

"Why shouldn't you handle him?" asked James.

"Because he will learn to rely on humans to feed him," explained Betty.

"What will you give him?" James asked. He peered into the cage. The owl blinked slowly at him.

"Well," Betty said thoughtfully. "I'll have to force-feed him at first. Owls mainly eat small mammals and birds in the woodlands. In the summer they hunt more in the open and catch rabbits, moles — even earthworms."

"I could go and dig up some worms," said James.

"I shouldn't worry just yet, James," Betty said. "He won't eat anything for a while. And he couldn't have worms for long. Owls need feathers and bones in their diet. I'll try to get some chicks from the chicken farm if they'll give them to me." She glanced at Dr. Emily. "This could be the last creature I'm able to help, I'm afraid, Mandy. The buildings are badly in need of repair and it's going to cost at least five hundred pounds to have them done."

"Five hundred pounds!" Mandy gasped.

"Yes," Betty said, shaking her head. "And to top it all, Sam Western's raised my rent. I simply don't have enough money to pay him, do the repairs, *and* feed the animals as well."

Sam Western was a local farmer who ran his large farm like a factory. He was well known for being both bad-tempered and mean. He was a tough businessman with no love for animals. He wouldn't care what happened to the waifs and strays at the sanctuary if it had to close.

Mandy's sadness turned to anger. "Why has Mr. Western done a mean thing like that?" she blurted.

"I think he wants the bungalow for one of his farm workers," Betty explained. "He knows I can't afford to pay him a higher rent."

"But you *can't* close down, Betty," Mandy said, almost in tears. "The sanctuary is your life!"

"I'm sorry, Mandy," Betty said, sounding close to tears herself. "I really don't have any choice."

"But what will happen to all the animals you've got here?" cried Mandy.

"I'll find homes for as many as possible," Betty said. "I've been in touch with the SPCA but they've told me they're overcrowded already. I'm afraid the rest will have to be destroyed."

It was just as Mandy had feared. "James and I are going to try to think of a way to get some money to help you," she said.

"That's right," James agreed, nodding his head vigorously.

Betty sighed. "I'm very grateful, you two, but I'm afraid it'll take more than your allowance to save this place."

"Oh, no," said Mandy. "I mean *raise* money like we do at school. We need to sit down and make a plan. Isn't that right, James?"

"Yup," James nodded fiercely. "We're going to do it as soon as we get back home."

"That's very kind of you," Betty said gratefully. "But five hundred pounds is an awful lot of money, I'm afraid."

"I'll give you my allowance to help pay for the owl's food." Mandy glanced at her mother with shining eyes. "That'll be OK, won't it, Mom?"

Dr. Emily patted her daughter's shoulder. "Yes, of course, Mandy, every little bit helps."

"So you'll be able to keep the baby owl here for now?" Mandy asked Betty.

Betty nodded. "Yes, I promise. I'll call the chicken farm right away. Perhaps you'd like to come back in a couple of days, Mandy, to see how he's doing?"

"You bet," said Mandy. "I wouldn't miss it for the world. Please try to hang on, Betty. We'll think of something; I know we will!"

*   *   *

Mandy and James left Dr. Emily talking to Betty and wandered outside.

In the paddock, Bubbles, a fat black Shetland pony with short legs, trotted up to the fence when he saw Mandy and James. Bubbles had been rescued by Betty when his owner's children had outgrown him. He put his nose through the rails and nuzzled Mandy's sleeve. With tears in her eyes, Mandy fondled his coarse forelock.

"I can't bear to think of it, James," she sniffed. "Poor old Bubbles might have to be put down."

"I know," James said glumly. "No one's going to want an old pony like him. That's why he's here in the first place."

"*I* would," Mandy said indignantly. "I'd love to have him." But in her heart she knew it was impossible. There was no room at Animal Ark to keep a pony, even one as small as Bubbles.

They left Bubbles and walked between the lines of dog kennels. Some were badly in need of repair. In one, a small mongrel jumped up at the wire when she saw them coming. The dog's name, Midge, was written on a plaque by the door.

"Hello, Midge." Mandy knelt to stroke the puppy. She wagged her tail, jumping up to try to lick Mandy's face through the wire.

Mandy stood up with a sigh. The dog whined pitifully as they walked away.

"Look," said Mandy. "There's old Clarence, that ram Betty saved from slaughter. And that Jersey heifer Sam Western was going to have killed because she's only got one eye."

"No one's going to want her, either," James said sadly. He stood on the bottom rail of the fence and scratched the top of the heifer's head.

"Come on," Mandy said with another sigh. "Let's go and sit in the car and try to think what we can do to help."

Dr. Emily came out of the office with Betty. "Thanks,

Betty," she said. "We'll come up again as soon as we can."

Mandy and James said their good-byes and climbed into the car. Blackie greeted them with a wildly wagging tail.

Mandy patted his head absentmindedly. There was no time to waste. If they don't think of something to save the sanctuary *soon*, it could quickly be too late!

"Why don't we just go and see Mr. Western?" Mandy suggested as they drove out of the gate. She turned to wave to Betty as she closed and locked the gate behind them. "We could just ask him not to raise the rent."

Dr. Emily shook her head. "Don't be silly, Mandy. You know what type of man he is. He's a businessman as well as a farmer. He won't care about stray animals. They're not worth two pennies to someone like him."

Mandy sighed. "It might be worth a *try.*"

"No, Mandy," Dr. Emily said firmly. "I can promise you it wouldn't."

On the way back to Animal Ark, Mandy and James tried to come up with a way to raise money.

"We could have a rummage sale," James suggested.

"Where would you hold it?" Dr. Emily asked.

"The village hall?" said James.

Dr. Emily glanced at them in the mirror. "It's usually

booked up ages in advance. I'm afraid Betty needs that money pretty urgently."

Mandy pulled a thoughtful face. "How about a swim-a-thon at school?" she said. Then her face fell. Swimming in the school's outdoor pool at this time of year wouldn't be any fun at all. Nobody was *that* silly. No, they had to think of something else.

"A sponsored bike ride?" James piped up. "Tons of people would do it. Your grandpa, for instance."

Mandy bit her lip. "That's not a bad idea, James. But we had one last semester, remember? People might not want to do one again so quickly."

"That's true," James said, raising his eyebrows.

All the way home, Mandy racked her brain. Most of her friends in the village were animal lovers. And most owned pets of one kind or another. She felt sure they would want to help. But it had to be more than just *giving* money. There were so many charities needing funds. The Reverend Hadcroft had started an appeal to repair the church roof. There was a big board by the church-yard gate with marks to show how much money had been raised. The marker was only up to two hundred pounds, so he needed lots more before work on the roof could even begin.

Someone from the village was always coming around collecting money for charities — guide dogs for the blind, the lifeboat men. They were all very good causes. If Mandy and James were going to get money for the sanctuary, it had to be something the villagers could really get involved in — something that would be fun *and* raise money at the same time. Something that had never happened in Welford before.

As Dr. Emily drove along the village main street with its pretty green in the center and old-fashioned shops, Mandy suddenly brightened.

"I know," she said. "Let's go see Grandma and Grandpa. They'll help us think of something."

"Good idea," said James. "Maybe your grandma's done some baking. All this thinking is making me hungry!"

Mandy's grandparents lived just up the road from Animal Ark, in a house called Lilac Cottage.

In the driveway, Mandy's grandpa was unloading plastic shopping bags from his new camper van. He looked delighted to see them.

"Come in and have a cup of hot chocolate!" he called.

Dr. Emily wound down her window. "I'd love to, Dad," she called to her father-in-law. "But I've got a few calls to make. These two want to pick your brain."

Grandpa ran his hand through his thatch of white hair. "What now?" he asked with a broad grin.

Mandy and James jumped out of the back. James opened the rear door for Blackie. Blackie ran up to

Grandpa and stuck his nose into one of the shopping bags.

"Blackie!" James shouted. He ran to grab the dog's collar.

"The animal sanctuary's going to have to close and we're trying to think of a way to save it — oh, Grandpa, you've got to help us!" Mandy said all in one breath.

Grandpa put his arm around her shoulders. "Now, calm down, Mandy. Help me with these bags and we'll go see what Grandma can find us to eat. No good thinking on an empty stomach." He waved to Dr. Emily. "See you later, Emily."

Dr. Emily put the car into gear and drove off down the street.

By now, Blackie had pulled out a bag of chips. It was clamped firmly between his teeth and he was shaking it to and fro, growling. James was desperately trying to get it away from him.

"I'm very sorry, Mr. Hope." James went red. Trust Blackie to embarrass him.

"Oh, let him have it," Mandy's grandfather said amiably. "It can be his morning snack."

James let go of the other end of the bag of chips and it suddenly burst all over the path. Blackie ran around gobbling up crumbs like a vacuum cleaner.

Laughing, Mandy and James helped Mr. Hope carry

the shopping indoors. They went up the garden path, under the budding lilac tree that gave the cottage its name, and in through the back door.

In the cozy kitchen, with its pine cupboards and bright red gingham curtains, Mandy's grandmother was putting groceries away in the pantry. The hot chocolate was already on the stovetop by the sink.

"Mandy, James, where did you come from?" Grandma exclaimed as they all came into the kitchen. She looked delighted to see them.

Mandy put the shopping bags on the kitchen table and ran to give her grandmother a hug. She loved coming to the cottage and chatting with her grandparents. Whenever she had a problem, they always seemed to find the answers.

"What's up, Mandy?" Grandma said, looking at her knowingly. She always seemed to sense when something was wrong.

Grandpa came in. "She's getting in a stew over the animal sanctuary," he said.

Over steaming mugs of hot chocolate and a plate of homemade cookies, Mandy and James told them the full story.

"So you see," Mandy said unhappily, "we've got to get a move on. And at the moment we just can't think of *anything*. Can we, James?"

James shook his head, his mouth too full to speak. Grandma and Grandpa looked glum.

"It's going to take a great deal of money to ensure the sanctuary stays open, Mandy," Grandpa said doubtfully. "Those places are expensive to run."

"I know, Grandpa," Mandy said, her eyes bright. "Betty needs five hundred pounds to repair the buildings right away. That's why we've got to think of something really original, something everyone will want to help with."

"I suggested a sponsored bike ride," said James.

"Great idea!" said Mandy's grandfather. He was an enthusiastic bike rider and could often be seen riding in the countryside surrounding the village.

"But we had one last semester," James went on. "Mandy said people won't want to do that again."

"That's probably true," said Grandpa, looking serious again. He looked at his wife expectantly. "Come on, Dorothy. You're usually full of ideas."

Mandy's grandmother was always campaigning for something or other; writing letters to Parliament, starting up petitions. Not long ago she'd saved the village post office from being closed down. This time, though, she seemed stumped.

Grandma took off her glasses and laid them on the table. She rubbed her eyes. "I know," she said suddenly. "How about a sponsored dog walk?"

"That's a good idea," said James. "Blackie would love that."

At the word "walk" Blackie's ears pricked up. He jumped up and put his front paws on the table. His tongue lolled out and his tail was wagging furiously.

"No, Blackie," James said patiently. "We're not going for a walk. Not now." He tried to push Blackie down but the dog refused to budge. He just barked and wagged his tail harder still.

Mandy laughed. "You'll have to stop saying that word, James."

"Down, Blackie!" James frowned, sneaking Blackie a piece of biscuit to make sure he did as he was told.

"It's a good idea, Grandma," Mandy went on. "But a dog walk would only involve people who own dogs."

"How about a *pet* walk?" said Grandma, putting her glasses back on. She said the word "walk" quietly so Blackie wouldn't hear.

Mandy giggled in spite of herself. "Oh, Grandma. I can't see anyone wanting to sponsor a tortoise! I want to get the whole village involved."

"Well . . ." Grandpa said slowly, "how about one of those shows? You know, where you get a prize for the best rabbit, the most obedient dog — that sort of thing." He brushed a crumb from his mustache. "Then even people with pet spiders will be able to take part." He sat back looking pleased with himself.

Mandy took a deep breath. What a terrific idea! Trust Grandpa to come up with a winner.

She jumped up from her chair and ran to give her grandfather a hug. "Oh, Grandpa, that's brilliant! We could have the best cat, the best hamster . . . even the best *rat*. We could call it the Grand Novelty Village Pet Show."

"Well," said her grandmother. "That does sound *very* grand indeed."

"It will be," Mandy said. "It will be the grandest event the village has ever seen. Oh, Grandpa, it's perfect!"

"I've got an idea," James said. He had been looking very thoughtful.

They all gazed at him expectantly.

"What?" asked Mandy.

"We could call our campaign SOS."

"SOS?" asked Grandpa, looking puzzled.

"Yup," said James smugly. "Save Our Sanctuary."

Mandy took one last gulp of hot chocolate and slammed her mug down on the table. She ran the back of her hand across her mouth. "Come on, James. Let's get back to Animal Ark. I'll call Betty to see if she thinks it's a good idea, too. Then we'll start making plans!"

Three

James hurriedly finished his cookie. He said good-bye to Mandy's grandparents and dashed after Mandy. She was already halfway down the road.

"Come *on*, James," she called over her shoulder. "There's no time to waste!"

When they arrived at Animal Ark, a woman dressed in old black Wellington boots and a brown jacket stood on the path outside the clinic door. She was desperately hanging on to the halter of a restless black goat. The goat had perky ears and a tail that waggled about as if it were on a spring. The woman was obviously having trouble holding him. The goat's delicate hooves clattered on the path like castanets.

It was Lydia Fawcett from High Cross Farm. She owned a herd of lively goats, and this one looked as if he was the liveliest of them all! But Lydia usually treated her animals with homemade remedies. She never came to the vets' unless something was seriously wrong. What on earth was she doing here?

Mandy ran up to her. "Hello, Lydia. Can I help?" she asked, almost laughing at the goat's antics. He certainly didn't look very sick.

Lydia twisted the halter in an effort to steady him. "Oh, yes, please, Mandy," she said. "Could you go in and get your father for me? Monty's got a really bad leg. I've tried to treat it myself but it's getting worse."

Mandy stared at the goat. He was leaping about on three legs like a ballet dancer. James stood at the gate, his hand over his mouth to try to stop himself laughing. He held tightly on to Blackie's leash. If Monty broke free, there was nothing Blackie liked better than a good game of chase.

"Hang on," Mandy said. "I'll go and get someone." She ran in through the clinic door.

Dr. Adam was writing up his notes from the morning

office hours. He looked up and gave a broad, lopsided grin as Mandy rushed in. "What's up?"

"Dad," Mandy said urgently, "Lydia's outside with Monty. I think you'd better go and see him before he causes havoc."

"Lydia?" Dr. Adam was already grabbing his bag. "It must be bad if she's dragged Monty all the way to the clinic!"

Outside, Lydia was till grappling with Monty. James was standing beside her looking helpless.

"Now, Lydia," Dr. Adam smiled kindly into Lydia's agitated face. "What's wrong with Monty?"

"He's got a nasty swelling on his back leg," Lydia said. "I tried to treat it myself but I'm afraid it's only gotten worse. *Monty!*" she said angrily. "Will you please have the good manners to stand still!" Monty ignored his mistress and went on bucking.

"Hmm," said Dr. Adam. "Let's have a look. Try to hold him still please, Lydia."

"I'm trying!" Lydia gasped.

Adam Hope couldn't help grinning. He turned to his daughter. "Give Lydia a hand, will you please, Mandy?"

Mandy put her arms around the goat's neck and gripped tightly. She murmured soothing words into his ear. "Nice Monty, good Monty. Now, let Dad take a look at that leg. He won't hurt you, I promise." The goat

tossed his head and rolled his eyes at her. Mandy tried her hardest to keep him steady.

Dr. Adam put his bag on the ground and bent to examine one of the animal's hind legs. Then he stood up, looking serious.

"I'm afraid he's got rather a nasty abscess. He's probably been kicked by one of the other goats. Go and ask Simon for the razor and some antibiotics, please, Mandy."

"OK, Dad." Mandy let go of Monty's neck and dashed back inside. She soon returned with the things her father wanted. Monty seemed to have calmed down a little and was standing still, trying to eat the hedge.

"Now, hold him steady," said Dr. Adam as Monty eyed him warily. He seemed to know just what Dr. Adam intended to do.

Mandy and James helped hold Monty still while Dr. Adam quickly shaved the hair from around the abscess.

"Hmm . . . nasty," Dr. Adam mumbled to himself. He took the hypodermic from its sterile package and inserted the point into a small bottle full of antibiotic. He drew the liquid into the body of the syringe. "OK," he said. "Here goes."

He skillfully injected the goat's flank so quickly Monty hardly seemed to notice. The animal didn't flinch. "There," said Dr. Adam, rubbing the spot where he had stuck the needle in. He stood back, looking satisfied. "He's as good as gold."

Then Dr. Adam took a small jar from his bag. "I'll just rub on this ointment to soothe it. There's no need to strangle him, Mandy. I'm sure he'll be fine now."

But Dr. Adam spoke too soon. As he rubbed on the ointment, Monty suddenly kicked out. Dr. Adam fell back in surprise, landing in a heap on the path. Mandy and James jumped sideways as the goat took to its heels and galloped off. Lydia was still hanging on to the halter. Blackie barked excitedly, doing his best to drag James after them.

"Thank you very much, Adam!" Lydia shouted over her shoulder, her black Wellingtons going like pistons.

By now, goat and owner were halfway across the village green. A line of churned-up turf showed where they had trampled across. Mandy and James collapsed into laughter.

"Are you OK, Dad?" Mandy spluttered as her father scrambled to his feet. He brushed the dirt from the seat of his jeans.

"Great," he said looking a bit dazed. "I don't know what Lydia feeds her goats — the same stuff racehorses eat, I wouldn't be surprised!"

Still laughing, all three of them went into Animal Ark. Mandy loved helping her father with his patients. It gave her a great feeling to know she'd had a hand in making them better.

Mandy and James followed Dr. Adam into the clinic and watched while he unpacked his bag and put the used syringe and bottle into the waste bin. He went to the sink and scrubbed his hands.

"Have you heard about Betty's sanctuary having to close?" Mandy asked, sobering up.

"Yes," Dr. Adam said grimly. "Your mom's been telling me the sad story. Have you decided what to do?"

"Yes," Mandy said, her eyes shining. "We're going to have a Grand Novelty Village Pet Show. I'm just going to call Betty and see what she thinks of the idea."

Dr. Adam raised his eyebrows. "Well, I think it's a great idea. Where are you going to hold it?"

Mandy glanced at James. She hadn't really thought about where they would hold the show. "On the village green, I suppose," she said. "And we'll need someone to judge the animals. You and Mom will do it, won't you, Dad?"

Dr. Adam looked affectionately at his daughter. "Oh, I think we could manage that."

"And we'll need prizes and tables and —" Mandy

broke off. She began to feel worried. It had suddenly dawned on her just how much organization was needed. But she was never one to refuse a challenge.

She jumped off the couch. "Come on, James. Let's go and call Betty. Then we'd better make a list of things we need to do."

"If you're having it on the green, you'll need permission from the parish council," Dr. Adam called as they rushed out.

Mandy came back, looking anxious. "Why?"

"Well, the green belongs to them. You can't just go holding things on it without permission."

"OK, then," said Mandy. "Who do I ask?"

"Mr. Markham," Adam Hope told her. "He's the chairman. He lives at number two, The Terrace. I went there yesterday, actually — his beagle had a litter of pups. They're a month old now and needed to be checked out."

"Oh, great!" Mandy said. "Maybe we'll be able to see them." There was nothing she loved more than a litter of puppies.

"Cynthia Markham's very proud of them," said Dr. Adam. "I'm sure she'll let you."

Mandy and James went into the house to telephone the sanctuary. Betty answered right away.

"Oh, Mandy, I think that's a really wonderful idea," she said when Mandy told her about the show. "If I can do anything to help, please let me know."

"How's the baby owl?" Mandy asked anxiously.

Betty hesitated, "I haven't been able to get him to eat anything yet, I'm afraid. I've dug up some worms but he won't take them."

Mandy's heart sank. "Oh, no. Maybe he's not hungry."

"I think he's still in a state of shock," Betty said. "A fall from that height's pretty traumatic. But he's alert and beady-eyed so I'm not too worried about him. He'll let me know when he's hungry."

"I'll come and see him as soon as I can," Mandy promised.

"Anytime," Betty said. "And let me know how plans are going for the show."

"We will." Mandy put the phone down with a sigh. Then she straightened up. It was pointless worrying about the owl. She knew Betty would do her best with him.

James was waiting in the hall with Blackie.

"Betty thinks the show's a great idea," Mandy told him. "Let's go and see Mr. Markham and find out if we can hold it on the green!"

*   *   *

The Terrace was a row of pretty Victorian cottages just off the lower main street. Number two had a green-painted front door.

Mandy went boldly up the steps and rang the door-bell. James tied Blackie to the gatepost and went to join her.

As the door opened, a chorus of barks and yelps came from the end of the long hallway. A gray-haired woman in pants and a long striped cardigan stood smiling at Mandy and James.

Mandy swallowed hastily. "Good morning," she said with a smile. "I'm Mandy Hope. Could we see Mr. Markham, please?"

Mrs. Markham knew right away who Mandy was. "Oh, you're the vets' daughter," she said, standing to one side. "Come in, come in. Have you come to see my Bunty's pups?"

Mandy bit her lip. "I'd love to," she told Mrs. Markham. "But could we see your husband first, please? It's very important."

"Yes, of course," Mrs. Markham said.

"Thanks," said Mandy. "This is my friend James Hunter."

James held out his hand solemnly. "How do you do," he said.

The woman shook his hand. "May I ask what you want to see my husband about?"

Mandy explained about their plan to raise money for the animal sanctuary.

Mrs. Markham looked impressed. "My, you two, you *are* good. Giving up your time to help Miss Hilder."

"It's for the sake of the animals," Mandy said. "They'll have to be put down and we can't bear the thought of it."

James shook his head. "That's right," he said. "Betty needs at least five hundred pounds, and we're going to get it for her."

"My, my, you are determined," Mrs. Markham's voice was full of admiration. She patted James's head as if he were six years old. James gave her a false kind of grin. "I'm sure my husband will help you if he can," Mrs. Markham went on. "Come this way, children."

Mrs. Markham led Mandy and James along the carpeted hallway. Through the kitchen door, Mandy spotted a beagle in a huge dog basket feeding a row of six plump puppies. Mandy let out her breath in delight as they passed.

Mrs. Markham ushered them into one of the back rooms. A tall, thin man with a bald head sat tapping away at an ancient typewriter. He turned as they entered and peered at them over the top of his glasses.

"These young people would like to have a word with you about something, Robert," Mrs. Markham explained. "I'll leave you to it."

Mandy turned to say thanks but Mrs. Markham had bustled away and shut the door behind her.

Mr. Markham looked Mandy and James up and down with a stern expression on his face. Mandy felt as if she were standing in front of the principal at school.

She had seen Mr. Markham before, walking through the village with a clipboard and pen, writing furiously as if he were making notes about everybody. She didn't know how old he was but he looked pretty ancient and *terribly* stern. She suddenly felt very nervous.

Mr. Markham continued peering at Mandy and James over the top of his spectacles. A frown creased his shiny brow. Then, suddenly, he took off his glasses and smiled. The smile seemed to change his whole face. Little blue eyes sparkled beneath his bushy eyebrows.

Mandy relaxed. Maybe this conversation wasn't going to be so bad after all!

"Well, young people" — Mr. Markham put his glasses down on the desk — "what can I do for you?"

Mandy explained all over again about the pet show and the animal sanctuary.

To their dismay, Mr. Markham shook his head. "I'm sorry," he said. "I'm afraid we just can't do it."

Mandy tried to hide her disappointment. "Why not?"

"It's because of that rummage sale the Young Farmers Club held at Eastertime, you see."

Mandy frowned. She didn't see at all. What did a rummage sale have to do with a pet show? They weren't *selling* pets, just showing them.

"The grass got so churned up," Mr. Markham explained, "that the parish council agreed it wouldn't let any more events be held there until next year. I'm sorry, young lady, but you'll have to find somewhere else to have your pet show. Unless you can wait until next year."

Mandy shook her head. "We can't. Betty Hilder needs the money *now.*"

Mr. Markham shook his head again. "Sorry. There's nothing I can do."

He stood up and went with them to the door. "If you do find somewhere suitable, let me know," he said. "I'd like to bring Bunty along. I'm sure she'd win a prize."

"Oh, yes, please do bring her," Mandy said enthusiastically. Trying to swallow her disappointment, she led the way along the hallway toward the kitchen, where Mrs. Markham was giving the beagle a drink of milk. The puppies were playing on the rug, barking and tumbling and having mock battles with one another.

"Come on in," she called to Mandy and James, who

were hesitating in the doorway. It didn't seem polite to go barging into the room without being asked.

Mandy went in and sat down on the floor. Seeing the litter of puppies had cheered her up.

"They're absolutely gorgeous," she said, holding one gently up to her cheek. She felt the warm, soft fur against her skin. The puppy squirmed and tried to get a mouthful of her hair. Mandy laughed and put him down with his brothers and sisters. He ran off, his roly-poly body wobbling, and disappeared under the kitchen table.

Mrs. Markham sighed. "Yes, I'll really miss them when they have to go."

"Have you found homes for them all?" asked James, playing tag with a puppy with a pretty brown face and floppy ears.

Mrs. Markham nodded. "Yes, I advertised them in the local paper. They were snapped up very quickly."

"Not like those poor dogs at the sanctuary," Mandy said sadly, getting up, ready to leave.

"Was my husband able to help you?" Mrs. Markham said as she went with them to the front door.

Mandy shook her head sadly. "No. He said an event like that would mess up the grass too much."

"Oh, dear," said Mrs. Markham. "I remember what the green looked like after that rummage sale last year. It was more like a plowed field than a village green. Did my husband have any other suggestions?"

Mandy shook her head again. "No, not really."

"I am sorry," Mrs. Markham said. "Let me know if you have any luck finding somewhere else." Then, suddenly, her face lit up. "I know," she said. "Why don't you ask Amelia Ponsonby?"

"Mrs. *Ponsonby*!" Mandy and James chorused.

"Yes," said Mrs. Markham. "Do you know her?"

Mandy and James stared at each other. They had had dealings with Mrs. Ponsonby before. In fact, there was hardly anyone in the village who *hadn't* had dealings with Mrs. Ponsonby one way or another. The woman made it her business to know everything and everyone in Welford!

"Do we *know* her?" James chuckled. "Everybody knows Mrs. Ponsonby."

"Well, then," said Mrs. Markham. "Why not ask her if you can have the show at her house? Bleakfell Hall is huge and it has a great big garden. I know Mrs. Ponsonby's very fond of animals. And she did adopt a dog from Betty's sanctuary. She might be willing to let you hold it there."

Mandy looked thoughtful. Maybe Mrs. Markham was right. Maybe Mrs. Ponsonby *would* let them hold the show at Bleakfell Hall.

But James looked dubious. "She's pretty fussy," he said.

"Well, it's up to you," said Mrs. Markham. "It could be worth a try."

They said good-bye. James untied Blackie from the gatepost and they headed off toward the village green.

"Well," said James, seeing Mandy's thoughtful face. "Are we going to ask Mrs. Ponsonby or not?"

"Yes," Mandy said matter-of-factly. "Remember when she adopted her little mongrel, Toby?"

"Yes," said James.

"Well, then we know she really cares about homeless animals. Come on, let's give it a try!"

Four

Mandy and James ran down the street and across the green toward Animal Ark, Blackie at their heels. They rushed around to the back to get their bikes.

Dr. Emily came to the gate. "Where are you two off to?"

"We're going up to Bleakfell Hall to ask Mrs. Ponsonby if we can hold the pet show there," Mandy explained hastily.

"Can I leave Blackie here, please?" James asked.

Dr. Emily took the Labrador's leash. "Yes, of course. I'll put him in the kitchen." She made a wry face. "Good luck with Mrs. Ponsonby — you're going to need it!"

"Thanks, Mom," said Mandy.

"And don't be a nuisance," Dr. Emily called as they pedaled away. "Mrs. Ponsonby's a very busy woman!"

They cycled pell-mell through the village. Outside the post office Mrs. McFarlane was talking to the postman.

"You two are in a hurry," she called as she saw Mandy and James speeding past.

"We're on urgent business," James called as they pedaled by.

Halfway up to Bleakfell Hall, Mandy's courage began to fail. She slowed down and waited for James to pedal alongside her.

"What do you think she'll say?" she asked, suddenly feeling they might be on a wild goose chase.

James bit his lip. "I don't know," he said. "She's awfully bossy. She might not give us a chance to tell her what it's all about."

"Yes, I know," said Mandy. Then she thought about Betty and the animals, and drew a deep breath. "Well," she said, "we're going to ask her. She won't bite our heads off, will she?"

"She might," said James. He had always been a little scared of Mrs. Ponsonby. She was so huge and had *such* a loud voice!

Mandy laughed at his dismal face and punched him playfully on the shoulder. "Be brave, James. Mrs. Ponsonby might be fussy but she's not a monster. Come on, I'll race you."

"If you say so," James mumbled.

Mandy sped on ahead. She pedaled over the bridge and through the stone gateway, then up the long gravel drive toward the imposing front door. Bleakfell Hall was a huge gray-stone Victorian mansion with tall chimneys and towers and turrets.

To Mandy's dismay, one wing was completely encased in scaffolding. Mrs. Ponsonby obviously had the builders in.

Mandy skidded to a halt on the gravel.

"Oh, no," she said disappointedly. "Builders!"

"She won't want to be bothered with us by the looks of it," said James, looking crestfallen.

Mandy took a deep breath. "Well, as we've come all this way, we might as well ask anyway." Mandy wasn't one to be easily put off.

They leaned their bikes against one of the stone pillars that flanked the front steps and went to press the old-fashioned doorbell beside the front door.

The housekeeper answered. She was a tiny woman in an apron almost to her ankles.

"Could we see Mrs. Ponsonby, please?" Mandy asked politely.

"Who shall I say is calling?" asked the housekeeper.

"Er . . . Mandy Hope and James Hunter," said Mandy.

"Please wait here!" The housekeeper scuttled away down a dim corridor toward the kitchen and disappeared inside muttering to herself.

After about five minutes Mrs. Ponsonby came sailing down the stairs in a tweed suit and sensible shoes. She wore a green felt hat with a feather in it over her blue-rinsed hair. Mrs. Ponsonby was very fond of her hats and had one to suit every occasion. In fact, Mandy couldn't remember ever having seen her in the same hat twice. Tucked under her arm was a pale-cream Pekingese with tiny black boot-bottom eyes. Scampering behind came Toby, a little brown mongrel. He ran up to Mandy and James, barking, his tail wagging furiously. He jumped up at Mandy. She bent down to stroke him.

"Hello, Toby," she said, tickling the little dog behind his ears. "You look well." She was pleased to see the little dog looking so healthy. When Betty Hilder had first brought Toby to Animal Ark, he had been abandoned with a broken leg.

Mrs. Ponsonby looked very surprised to see them standing there. She peered at them through the lenses of her pink glasses.

"Who on earth let you in?" she said loudly.

"Er . . . a lady. I think she was a housekeeper," said

Mandy in a small voice. She gazed up at Mrs. Ponsonby. The woman looked larger than ever, standing above Mandy, staring down at her.

Mrs. Ponsonby frowned and sighed. "That woman is hopeless, isn't she?" she said, more to the Pekingese than to Mandy and James. "She's probably forgotten all about you already. You could have been standing here all day." She reached the bottom stair. "Well, what can I do for you?" she asked. "I'm afraid I can't cope with any more dogs, Mandy."

"Oh, no," Mandy assured her hastily. "It's not that. It's something else."

"Well?" Mrs. Ponsonby raised her eyebrows.

Mandy straightened up. "We came here to ask you a favor," she said with determination.

Mrs. Ponsonby looked suspicious. "A favor?"

"Yes," Mandy said breathlessly. Then she quickly explained their scheme.

Mrs. Ponsonby put Pandora down on the floor. The Pekingese waddled off.

"Pandora!" called Mrs. Ponsonby. "Pandora, come back!"

Toby followed the peke. They both ignored their mistress.

When Mandy finished explaining, Mrs. Ponsonby shook her head. The feather on her hat waved around just like Pandora's tail. "I couldn't possibly let everyone run riot on my property."

"They won't run riot," James said. "We'll have things properly organized. Dr. Adam and Dr. Emily are going to help, and I'm sure my mom and dad will, too."

Mrs. Ponsonby shook her head again. "No. It's bad enough with the builders and their huge boots. I'm afraid you'll have to find someplace else. I'd like to help but it's impossible." She looked at them kindly. "I'd be pleased to enter Pandora and Toby." She sniffed. "Of course, they'll win every class they enter."

Mandy sighed and tried not to look too disappointed. "Oh, well, thanks, Mrs. Ponsonby. We'll just have to find someplace else."

Mrs. Ponsonby escorted them to the door. "I was just going to see Mr. Western about all the mud his tractors leave on the road," she said. "My car gets *filthy* when I drive past his place. I *could* have a word with him about Miss Hilder's rent. You said he's raised it?"

"Yes," Mandy said mournfully. "And Betty can't possibly afford to pay it and have the animal shelters repaired *and* buy food as well."

"I'll have to find out what's going on," said Mrs. Ponsonby. She liked to know everyone's business. "Goodbye, children," she called as they walked forlornly down the steps.

Mandy and James got on their bikes and rode slowly down the driveway.

"She didn't even say she was sorry," James said grumpily.

"I know," Mandy said with a sigh. She felt really sad. Would they ever find anywhere to hold the show? "Oh, James," she said miserably. "*Now* what are we going to do?"

"Go home and think," said James.

Mandy and James arrived back at Animal Ark and sat around the kitchen table drinking Cokes.

"We could ask our principal if we could have the pet show at school," James suggested hopefully.

Mandy shook her head. "That's no good. We want the show here in the village. It's the *Welford* sanctuary. It's got to be the *Welford* show."

James scratched his ear. "Hey," he said suddenly. "What about the Parker Smythes? They've got a great big garden *and* an indoor swimming pool — we could have dog swimming races!"

Mandy made a face. "The Parker Smythes? I don't think that's a very good idea. You know how stuck-up they are."

"Well," said James, "Mrs. Parker Smythe loves showing off. You know she does. If we held the show there, everyone in the village would be able to see her fancy house and her fancy swimming pool, wouldn't they?"

"Hmm . . ." said Mandy. "That's true. I hadn't thought of that."

"And she loves bragging about Mr. Parker Smythe being a television producer," James went on. "She could tell everyone that, too."

Mandy decided it was worth a try. She jumped up. "OK, James. You've convinced me! Let's go and ask."

The Parker Smythes lived in Beacon House, a huge white mansion set high up on Beacon Hill. It looked down on the rest of the village just as Mrs. Parker Smythe looked down on its inhabitants.

Mandy and James rode up there in no time at all.

Outside the mansion's high security gates, Mandy's heart sank. The sign saying TRESPASSERS WILL BE PROSE-CUTED seemed a bad omen. Maybe it had been a mistake to come here. The huge gates and the sign hardly welcomed people to the house.

Mandy sat astride her bike with her feet on the ground. She looked at James. "What do you think?"

James shrugged and took off his glasses. He polished them on the knee of his jeans, then put them back on. "I don't know," he said.

Mandy chewed her lip. It was really important that they got the pet show organized as soon as possible.

They had to find somewhere to have the show. This could be their very last chance.

Mandy combed her hair back with her fingers and squared her shoulders determinedly. She had made up her mind to give it a try.

"Well," she said to James. "Here goes!"

She stood on tiptoe and pressed a button on the security intercom attached to one of the pillars. There was a hiss and a popping noise, then a squeaky voice asked who was there.

Mandy told the machine and after another click the huge gates swung silently open. It was like getting permission to enter a prison!

Mandy and James biked along the driveway, past the rows of trees and between neat hedges that led up to the front door. Their ring on the bell was answered right away.

A short, overweight girl stood dwarfed by the huge door frame. She was dressed in bright pink Lycra leggings and a white fluffy sweater with a kitten embroidered on the front. She had chocolate all around her mouth.

"Yes?" she asked. "Have you come to play with me?" Her tongue came out as she tried to lick the chocolate off.

"Hi, Imogen," Mandy said cheerfully. Imogen was the spoiled seven-year-old daughter of the Parker Smythes.

"Is your mom home?" James piped up.

"She's in the sauna," said Imogen, as if taking a sauna were the most ordinary thing in the world.

"A sauna!" James spluttered beside Mandy.

Mandy nudged him. There was only one way to deal with Imogen and that was to be as sweet as pie.

"Do you have any idea how long she'll be?" she asked the little girl gently.

Imogen wriggled around as if she had ants in her pants. "Yes," she said. "Years, probably. She and Daddy went to a party last night and Mommy's recovering."

"Oh," said Mandy, not knowing what else to say.

"But come in and play with me," Imogen insisted. "My daddy bought me a new dollhouse, and I've got a new video and lots of —"

Just then Mrs. Parker Smythe came into the hallway. Mandy sighed with relief. She'd thought Imogen would never stop.

Mrs. Parker Smythe was swathed from head to immaculately painted scarlet toenails in a pure white, fluffy robe. Her blonde hair was covered by a peach-colored turban.

"Who is it, Immie darling?" she inquired.

"Mandy Hope and James Hunter," Imogen replied. "They've come to play with me."

"Er . . . no," Mandy said. "Sorry, we actually wanted to see your mom."

Imogen stuck out her bottom lip in a sulk. "It's not fair," she moaned. "No one ever comes to play with me."

"I'm not surprised," James whispered to Mandy.

Mrs. Parker Smythe tottered toward them across the marble floor. She wore white satin high-heeled mules that slipped and slithered as if the floor were covered with ice.

She stared at Mandy. "You're the vets' daughter, aren't you?"

"Yes," Mandy confirmed. She went on talking quickly. She knew if she let Mrs. Parker Smythe get a word in edgewise, she would hear endless stories about her husband's involvement in television, the famous people that came to stay in Beacon House, and stories of how brilliant Immie was at all kinds of things from playing the piano to tap dancing.

When Mandy finished telling Mrs. Parker Smythe why they were there, the woman sat down heavily on one of the gold brocade chaise longues that lined the sparkling hallway.

"I'm not sure my husband would relish the idea of the hoi polloi coming up here in droves," she said.

"What's hoi polloi?" James whispered in Mandy's ear.

"I've no idea," Mandy whispered back.

Mrs. Parker Smythe looked at them as if they were something that had crawled out of the woodwork. "Hoi polloi," she said, obviously overhearing. "Villagers . . . you know, *common* people."

"But wouldn't you love them to see your gorgeous house?" said Mandy. "And your lovely garden. Your husband could even make a movie of the event." She turned to Imogen, "You could be the star, Imogen."

Imogen began to jump up and down, waving her fat fists in the air. "Yes, Mommy, yes, Mommy, yes, Mommy," she chanted.

Mrs. Parker Smythe passed her hand across her eyes. "Immie darling, I've got the most dreadful headache." She looked slightly bewildered.

Imogen ran up to her and banged her on the knee. "I want the pet show here!" she shouted. "I want to be a movie star!"

Mandy glanced at James and could see he was tempted to throw darling Immie into the Parker Smythes' indoor swimming pool.

Mrs. Parker Smythe was trying to calm her daughter down. "Very well, dear," she was saying. "We'll have the pet show if that's what you want." She glanced up at Mandy and James. "But it will have to be sweet little

bunnies and kittens and things like that. I can't have great big dogs trampling over my beautiful Persian rugs."

"The animals wouldn't have to come indoors," Mandy assured her.

Mrs. Parker Smythe waved her hand. "Well, they might make messes on the lawn. We've got the famous Italian film director Mario Ponti coming next week. Can you imagine him treading . . ." She shuddered. "I couldn't take the risk. Just bunnies and kitties."

"And mice?" James asked innocently.

Mandy almost laughed out loud. At the mention of the word "mice" Mrs. Parker Smythe gave a little scream. Her turban wobbled and slipped to one side. "Mice! You aren't serious?"

Mandy couldn't resist taking it further. "Oh, yes," she said. "If it's only going to be *small* pets, there'll be mice, gerbils, spiders, rats . . ."

For one minute Mandy thought Mrs. Parker Smythe was going to faint. She went almost as pale as her robe. They'd blown their chances of holding the pet show at Beacon House, that was for sure!

Mrs. Parker Smythe stood up shakily and took hold of Mandy's and James's elbows. She steered them quickly to the front door. "No, I'm sorry," she breathed. "I think perhaps you'd better find somewhere else to

have your pet show. I'd be quite happy to give a donation to the sanctuary." She shuddered again. "But
mice . . . and *rats* . . . oh, dear, I feel quite faint. I think
I'll go have a nap."

She pushed Mandy and James out the door and shut
it firmly behind them. In the hall, Imogen began to
shout and scream, "I want mice, I want mice, I want
mice!"

James took the lead. He grabbed Mandy's arm.
"Come on, let's go."

Still giggling, they tore off down the drive. The huge
gates opened as if by magic, and they were through,
pedaling back down the hill toward the village. Mandy
threw back her head and laughed. Mrs. Parker Smythe's
expression when they mentioned the mice had been so
funny!

"Did you see her face?" Mandy chuckled. "Poor Mrs.
Parker Smythe, she'll have nightmares for a week.
Whose idea was it to go there, James?"

"Mine," James said sheepishly. "Sorry."

Mandy stopped her bike and looked at the wide
sweep of moorland and the blue sky with just a few cot-
ton-ball clouds drifting slowly across the tops of the
hills. She heaved a sigh. She felt disappointed. But holding a pet show at Beacon House would never have
worked. They'd just have to find somewhere else.

"It's OK, James," she said. "We're not giving up yet. Come on. Let's get back and see what other bright ideas we can come up with."

When they reached the village, James went into the McFarlanes' store to get some sodas while Mandy waited outside. When James came out, they parked their bikes by the village bench and sat down. The village bench was always a good place to sit and think. Mandy's mind was racing. They'd tried three things now and nothing was working out. She began to feel desperate. Someone, somewhere, must be willing to host the show.

The Reverend Hadcroft came riding down the road on his old black bicycle. He went into the McFarlanes' store and came out with the daily paper under his arm.

"Hello, you two," he called. "You look down in the dumps."

"We are," James called.

The vicar strolled over and sat beside them. He was a young man with a shock of black hair and bright blue eyes.

"OK," he said. "Tell me what's up."

Between them they told him their story.

Mr. Hadcroft frowned and fiddled thoughtfully with the edge of his cassock. "It seems to me," he said wisely, "that you two are making a mountain out of molehill."

A mountain out of molehill! Mandy thought indignantly. At this moment saving the animal sanctuary was just about the most important thing in the world!

"What do you mean?" she asked, puzzled.

The vicar grinned broadly. "Well," he said, "why not hold it in the vicarage garden? If it's good enough for the Welford Women's Club to hold their summer fair, then it's good enough for you to hold a pet show, isn't it?"

Mandy's heart leaped. The vicarage garden would be excellent! It had a big square lawn with lots of places to put tables and mark out parade rings. It would be just perfect.

"Oh, wow, Mr. Hadcroft," she said excitedly. "Could we?"

Mr. Hadcroft grinned. "Yes, why not?"

Mandy leaped to her feet. "Oh, that would be really great. Thanks, Mr. Hadcroft." She felt like hugging him but wasn't quite sure if it would be the right thing to do. She turned to James, her eyes shining. "Come on, James. There's lots to do." They were going to have an incredibly busy spring break, that was for sure!

There was a twinkle in the vicar's eye as he stood up with them. "Of course," he said, "I'll need a donation for the church roof fund if I'm going to let you use my garden."

Mandy's face fell. She knew how badly the church needed a new roof, but animals needed roofs over their heads, too. "Oh . . ." she said, trying not to sound too disappointed. She winced. "How much?"

The vicar clasped his hands together in front of him and raised his eyes to the sky as if he were asking for guidance. Finally he looked at Mandy and James.

"Shall we say one pound? Could you handle that?"

Mandy stared at him. Then a huge grin broke over her face. When it came to teasing, Mr. Hadcroft was as bad as her dad!

She flashed him a smile. "I'm sure we could handle a pound, aren't you, James?"

"Absolutely," said James.

"Great!" exclaimed Mr. Hadcroft. "You'd better come and see me later when you've made some more plans. I'll do anything to help you, of course."

"We will," Mandy called as they pedaled their bikes hurriedly toward Animal Ark. All of a sudden she felt wonderful. She might have known they would succeed in finding someplace. In a village like Welford, there was always *someone* to lend a helping hand.

Mandy's mind was already whirling, planning their next move. She wanted to make the Grand Novelty Village Pet Show an event that no one would ever forget!

Five

Mandy and James dashed excitedly back toward Animal Ark to tell the Hopes the good news. Mandy was already thinking up ideas. They'd need tables, prizes, someone to —

Suddenly a green car swung around the corner. At the same time, it seemed from out of nowhere, a beautiful tan-and-black German shepherd streaked across the village green. It ran right into the road. There was nothing the car driver could do to avoid it. There was a loud, ominous screech of brakes and a sickening thud as the front bumper hit the dog.

Mandy skidded to a halt and dropped her bike. Her

hands flew to her mouth. For a moment she froze in horror.

"Oh, no!"

Heart thudding with fear, Mandy sprang forward. The dog was lying motionless on its side in the road. The driver, a woman in her twenties, had gotten out and was standing looking at it, shaking her head. Tears were running down her face. She wrung her hands together in despair.

"It just ran out. There was nothing I could do!" the woman wailed.

"I know," Mandy gasped. "I saw. Don't worry. It wasn't your fault."

The young woman looked at Mandy with an agonized expression on her face. She knelt down beside the unconscious dog. "What on earth should we do?"

Then a young man in a black leather jacket appeared from around the corner. He had longish, thick blond hair and a tanned face with startling blue eyes. "Sheba!" he shouted desperately. "Sheba!"

His eyes widened in horror when he saw what had happened.

He rushed over and knelt down beside Mandy. He rocked backward and forward on his heels. There were tears in his eyes as he glanced at her.

"She ran away from me," he said, looking distraught.

"I'm so sorry," the young woman said, wiping her eyes. "I couldn't avoid her. She just ran out."

"I saw it all," Mandy said quickly. "Nothing could have been done to stop it."

The young man stretched out his hand to touch the dog.

"No, don't touch her!" Mandy said hastily. Her mind was racing. The dog was still breathing but unconscious. There was no sign of any blood, but it would be a mistake to touch or move Sheba until either Dr. Adam or Dr. Emily had taken a look at her.

Mandy quickly shrugged off her jacket. She laid it very gently over the animal. "I'll get help." She turned to James. "Don't let anyone move her," she said urgently.

Then Mandy was off, racing toward Animal Ark, her heart pounding. She knew the rules of first aid. Keep the animal warm, look for signs of bleeding, of broken limbs. But her mom or dad were the ones to help. People who didn't know what they were doing might do more harm than good.

Mandy flew in the clinic door. It hit the wall with a bang.

Jean Knox was just about to protest when she saw Mandy's white face.

"Where's Mom or Dad?" Mandy cried.

"In the house . . ." Jean began. But Mandy had already disappeared. She dashed through the clinic and into the kitchen.

Dr. Adam was ironing his white veterinarian's coat. He looked up in surprise as Mandy ran in.

"Dad, quick. A dog's been hit by a car!"

Dr. Adam quickly switched off the iron and ran to get a blanket and his bag. He sped down the path after Mandy.

In the road, James was standing with his arms out to warn any oncoming traffic. For once, Blackie sat obediently by his feet. The young man was talking to James.

"My uncle will kill me!" he said. He sat on the curb with his head in his hands.

"Your uncle?" asked James, waving a motorcyclist past.

"Yes, I'm staying with him at Moon Cottage. Sheba's his dog. I begged him to let me take her out. I love dogs, but I live in the city, and you can't keep a dog in an apartment."

Mandy arrived just in time to hear him explaining. Her heart lurched with sympathy. She knew how hard it was to control a dog like a German shepherd if you weren't used to it.

The young man looked up. Relief crossed his face when he saw Dr. Adam's leather bag.

"This is my dad," explained Mandy, "He's a vet. Sheba will be OK now, don't worry."

But Mandy sounded more confident than she felt. The dog was still unconscious and her breathing was shallow. One hind leg lay at a crooked angle. Mandy could only pray it wasn't broken. Then, horrified, she noticed blood seeping from Sheba's lower jaw. Her stomach turned over. "Dad!" she cried. "Look!"

Dr. Adam's face was grim as he knelt down beside the unconscious animal. He took out his stethoscope and listened to the dog's heart and lungs.

"They seem OK," he said, sounding relieved. He replaced the stethoscope, then gently lifted the dog's upper lip and pressed a finger against her gum. When he took it away, the gum immediately went pink again, although his finger was covered in blood.

Dr. Adam looked up. "If the gum hadn't turned pink," he explained, "it would have meant she had internal bleeding. Luckily that seems OK. The blood's from where her teeth have pierced her lip." He pulled the dog's eyelids open and looked into her pupils. "She's definitely in shock. Let's hope that's all."

He quickly examined the dog's limbs. "Umm," he muttered, touching the crooked hind leg. "I spoke too soon. This one's broken, I'm afraid. Let's get her back to the clinic before she wakes up."

Mandy helped her dad spread the blanket out on the road.

"Help me," Dr. Adam said to the young man. "And be careful," he warned. "If she comes around, she might bite."

Gently supporting the dog's head and body, they lifted her onto the blanket to use it as a makeshift stretcher. Dr. Adam made sure the dog's neck was extended so her breathing wasn't obstructed.

Mandy and James trailed behind as Dr. Adam and the young man carried Sheba over to Animal Ark.

"Poor Sheba," James said mournfully.

"If it's just a broken leg, she'll be OK," said Mandy. "Dad'll put it in a cast and then keep her at the Ark to make sure there's nothing worse wrong with her."

Back at Animal Ark, Mandy and James sat in the waiting room with the young man. In the clinic, Dr. Adam and Simon gave Sheba a more thorough examination and put her leg into a cast.

The young man introduced himself. "I'm Mark Boston," he said. "I'm looking for a house to buy in Welford. It's such a great place." He shook his head. "I don't know if my uncle will want me living near him after this."

Mandy tried to cheer him up. "It really wasn't your fault," she insisted. She suddenly realized she hadn't seen the car driver since she had rushed to get her dad. "What happened to the woman driving the car?"

"She had to pick up her kids from school," Mark explained. "She said she'd call later to see how Sheba was. She felt terrible."

"So did I," James piped up. "I thought Sheba was dead."

"Don't even think about it!" Mark shook his head. He turned to Mandy. "I don't know what I'd have done without your help, Mandy. I'm really grateful."

Mandy shrugged. "It's a good thing we were there," she said, "I'd have done the same for any animal." Her face lit up. "I want to be a vet, too."

"Well, I'm sure you'll make a great one."

Just then, Dr. Adam came in, drying his hands on a towel.

Mark jumped up anxiously. Dr. Adam put a reassuring hand on his arm. "Now, don't panic. She's going to be OK."

Mandy felt relief wash over her. Mark looked relieved, too. He sat down again, heavily. Color flooded back into his cheeks. "Is it just her leg?"

"I'm pretty sure that's all that's wrong with her, but I'll keep her under observation. You'd better go and tell your uncle what's happened."

Mark made a worried face. "He's going to kill me," he repeated. "I know he is."

"We'll come with you if you want," volunteered Mandy. "We can tell him it wasn't your fault."

Mark smiled down at her. "The thing is, Mandy, it *was* my fault. I should have had her on the leash." He sighed. "No, I've got to face the music." Then he laughed loudly, although Mandy didn't see what was so funny.

Mark went on. "If I do come to live near here," he said, "I want a house with lots of land so I can keep some animals. You two will have to come and give me a few hints on how to look after them."

"We'd love to," Mandy said. She liked Mark a lot. Anyone who liked animals was OK in Mandy's book. And, it was very strange, she had the feeling that she'd seen Mark somewhere before.

"Excellent," James said with a grin. He patted Blackie. "You can practice on Blackie if you want."

Mark smiled. "I think I'd better have a few lessons first."

"Have you been to Welford before?" Mandy asked. She was still trying to think where she might have seen him.

Mark nodded. "Years ago, when I was a kid about your age. I never forgot what a great place it was. I always had this dream of living in the country, and now I've got the money to do just that."

They went through to see Sheba. She was awake now, sitting on the floor, licking her newly plastered leg. She looked groggy and very sorry for herself.

"I've given her a sedative," said Dr. Adam. "She's bound to be bruised and sore. We'll put her out in the recovery room."

"Will she try to get the cast off?" asked Mark.

"She might," said Dr. Adam. "If she keeps on biting it, we'll have to put a plastic cone over her head so she can't reach it. Let's see how she does first. Some dogs accept the cast in no time at all and hop around as if they've worn it all their lives."

Mark crouched down and fondled Sheba's head. She managed a feeble wag of her tail.

"I'm sorry, old girl," Mark said, his voice breaking. After a minute or two he stood up, squaring his broad shoulders. "I'm sure Clive, my uncle, will want to come and see her. Is that OK?"

"Of course," said Dr. Adam. "And it'll probably be OK to pick her up this time tomorrow."

Mark shook his head. "Thanks, I'm really grateful."

"Just part of the job," Dr. Adam said. "It's lucky

Mandy was there. If anyone had tried to move Sheba it could have caused more injury."

"I know," Mark said. He put his arm around Mandy and gave her a hug. "I'll buy you a Coke sometime, Mandy, and you, James."

Dr. Adam walked out with Mark, discussing fees. "I'll pay, of course," Mark was saying.

Mandy stood watching. Then a frown creased her brow. She chewed her lip. "You know, James," she said thoughtfully. "I've seen Mark somewhere before."

"If he came to stay in the village you might have seen him then," James suggested.

"Maybe," said Mandy. "But I'd have been a little kid. No, I've seen him recently but I just can't think where!"

When the excitement and worry of the injured dog was over, Mandy and James sat at the kitchen table with pencil and paper, making plans for the Grand Novelty Village Pet Show.

"We'll need to make some fliers," said James. He was good at that kind of thing.

"Yes," Mandy agreed. It was vital that as many people as possible knew when and where the show would be held.

"But when *are* we going to have it?" asked James. "We haven't decided yet."

"Saturday's best," said Mandy. "When people don't have to work."

"Right," said James. "Next Saturday?"

"Yes," she said quickly. "Let's make it next Saturday!"

"We'd better ask Mr. Hadcroft if that day's OK," said James.

"Good idea," Mandy jumped up. "I'll call him now."

She came back smiling. "Saturday's fine," she said. "Mr. Hadcroft wondered if we'd have everything organized in time, but I said we would."

"Great," said James. "Let's make that list. First we'll need prizes."

Mandy gulped. "Prizes! Of course. Where are we going to get those from?"

James bit the end of his pencil. "Um . . . I don't know."

"I could ask Walter Pickard. He loves animals. He might find something we could give as a prize."

"OK," James scribbled away. "We could walk around the village and ask people if they'll donate a prize. Does that sound like a good idea?"

"Great idea," said Mandy. "I'm sure there are lots of people who'll give something."

"Good," said James. "Now we need to decide what competitions we're going to have. Then we'll need tables and cages and judges and a loudspeaker and . . ."

Mandy stared at him. Tables, cages . . . It looked as if finding the venue and prizes were only the first of a long line of problems they had to solve.

The door opened and Simon came into the kitchen. "What's this?" he asked, peering over James's shoulder.

"A list of stuff we need for our pet show," said James.

"You haven't got 'tent' on it," said Simon.

Mandy gulped. "What do we need a tent for?"

"In case it rains, of course. You can't trust the weather this time of year. You can't parade animals around in the pouring rain. They'll end up looking like drowned rats."

Mandy's face fell. Simon was right. She hadn't thought of that. Where on earth were they going to get a tent from?

"The scouts have one!" James said suddenly. "Maybe they'd let us borrow it."

"It will cost you tons of money," said Simon.

Mandy looked at him sideways. She had already promised her allowance to Betty for the owl's food. Where on earth was she going to get the money to rent a tent? Then she noticed Simon was grinning. "You're joking, aren't you?"

"Well, maybe not tons of money but they do charge to rent it out."

Mandy sighed. This was all becoming very complicated. But she wasn't going to get discouraged. Grandma always said nothing was worth doing unless it was worth doing well.

"Anyway," said Simon, "why don't you ask Jean? She's friends with Mrs. Browne, the scout leader. She might put in a good word for you."

"Great, thanks, Simon. If she's Jean's friend she might let us have it for nothing!" Mandy was going to jump up to ask Jean that very minute, but James held her arm.

"Hang on," he said. "Let's get this list done."

Mandy sat down again. "OK — what next?"

"The competitions."

Mandy raised her eyebrows thoughtfully. "Right . . . er, how about the dog with the waggiest tail?"

Simon laughed when he heard Mandy's suggestion.

"I guess Blackie would win that," Simon said as he walked toward the door. "You've got to give everyone a fair chance, you know. No favoritism."

"We will," Mandy said indignantly. "That's why we're having all kinds of different classes."

"How about the cat with the longest whiskers," Simon suggested.

James scribbled away. "Great. What else?"

"I'm sure you two will think of something," Simon said. He pushed the door open. "If you need any more suggestions, let me know."

"Thanks, Simon," Mandy said. She was still racking her brains. What kind of pets did her village friends have?

There were cats and dogs, of course. Old Ernie Bell, who lived near Mr. Pickard, had a pet squirrel. There were rabbits and guinea pigs, and she knew of at least two school friends who kept rats as pets. Mandy chuckled. She only had to think of the word "rat" and she could see the chocolate-covered Imogen Parker Smythe and her poor mother's expression of horror.

There were bound to be other pets as well. Pets like budgies, parrots, stick insects, goldfish. The list was endless.

"How about the rodent with the twitchiest nose," she suggested to James. "That'll cover gerbils, hamsters, mice, and *rats!*"

"*Rats!*" James screeched, imitating Mrs. Parker Smythe, "Oh, no, not *rats!*"

Mandy laughed. "What else can you think of? We're not getting very far."

"How about the most disobedient dog?" he suggested, pushing his glasses back up his nose.

"You're thinking of Blackie again," said Mandy.

James looked indignant. "No, I'm not. What about Pandora and Toby? Did you see the way they ignored Mrs. Ponsonby this morning?"

Mandy grinned. "I certainly did. Those dogs are wonderful at ignoring Mrs. Ponsonby. They're the only ones who can!"

James laughed. "Should I put that on the list, then?"

Mandy nodded. "Sure, yes, go ahead. It'll be much more fun than the most *obedient* one. And that's what we want — people to have . . . fun!"

James was scribbling furiously. "What else? We need about ten in all."

"The most talkative budgie?" suggested Mandy.

"Excellent," said James, adjusting his glasses again. Mandy looked thoughtful. "Hmm . . ."

"The stickiest stick insect?" James suggested.

"Now you *are* being silly," Mandy laughed.

The list was growing rapidly — the best rescued dog or cat, the best groomed pet, the most unusual pet.

"My friend at school has a pet wood louse," said James. "I bet that would win."

To round it off they decided on the dog who can eat his dinner fastest and the most scruffy pet in Welford.

They sat back looking pleased with themselves.

"Now," said Mandy. "The prizes."

"And someone to present them," added James.

Mandy bit her lip. She'd forgotten all about that. What they needed was someone famous. Someone who would really draw the crowds. Who on earth could they find? Suddenly, she had an idea. "What about Susan Collins's mom?"

Susan and Mrs. Collins lived in a big house on the road to Walton. Mrs. Collins used to act in *Parson's Close*, a soap opera on TV, and still did a little acting from time to time. Her professional name was Miranda Jones.

James's eyes lit up. "Perfect! Give her a call!"

She hurried out into the hall to use the phone. Minutes later, she came back looking crestfallen.

"She said she'd love to, but she's got to visit her aunt in the hospital on Saturday."

James stuck his elbows on the table. "Never mind," he said. "Maybe we'll think of someone else. I'll go home now and do the fliers. Then we'll take them around the village tomorrow and ask people about prizes."

"Good idea," said Mandy. "I can't wait!"

Six

Just as James was going out, there was a knock at the back door.

When Mandy opened it, a tall man with black hair and a beard stood on the step. He looked very stiff and stern but when he spoke he had a kind and gentle voice. He wore jeans and an open-necked shirt with a bright scarf tied at the collar.

Although he was a relative newcomer to the village, Mandy had seen the man several times before. He was a painter, and he often sat down by the river with his brushes and easel or on the village green, painting watercolor pictures of the houses and church.

"My name is Clive Moon," he said, sounding very apologetic. "I'm sorry, the clinic seems to be closed, but I wondered if I may see my dog? She was hit by a car when my nephew was taking her for a walk."

"Oh, yes, please come in. I'll take you to the recovery room," said Mandy. "The clinic doesn't open again until six, except for emergencies." She waved good-bye to James and then took Mr. Moon to the recovery room. Simon was there, checking up on Sheba.

Mr. Moon put out his hand. "How do you do, young man. Is my dog going to be all right?" he asked Simon anxiously. He bent to caress the sleeping dog.

"Yes, she's going to be fine," Simon reassured him. "She'll be stiff for a while, of course. And she'll have to get used to walking on three legs while she has the cast, but it's amazing how adaptable dogs can be."

"Is Mark OK?" Mandy asked. "He was really upset."

Mr. Moon looked up at her, then got to his feet. "Yes, he's recovered now. I know it wasn't his fault. People drive far too quickly through this village. One day someone's going to get killed. Were you the young lady who ran for the vet?"

Mandy nodded, feeling a little shy. "He's my dad."

"Yes, so I've heard." Mr. Moon put out his hand for her to shake. "I wanted to thank you. Mark said if it hadn't been for you, Sheba might have perished."

Mandy almost giggled. Mr. Moon made Sheba sound like an old balloon. But instead she blushed and couldn't think of anything to say.

"She's wonderful with animals," said Simon.

"Yes." Mr. Moon gazed at Mandy. He had piercing eyes that seemed to look right through her. "I can see that. You will make a good vet yourself one day, young lady."

"That's what I want to be," Mandy said, losing her shyness. Mr. Moon was very friendly in a funny, old-fashioned kind of way.

"Well, I wish you good luck," said Mr. Moon. He took another look at Sheba, then Mandy saw him out.

"Dad will let you know when it's OK for her to go home," she said.

"Good-bye, young lady," he said. "I look forward to seeing you again." His funny, formal way of speaking made Mandy smile.

Mr. Moon strode off down the path. He stopped by the gate to smell one of the blossoms on the rhododendron by the gate. He examined it closely, then went off muttering to himself.

Mandy went back to Animal Ark to do her chores before dinner. What an exciting day it had been. She swept the floor and tidied up — putting empty plastic wrappers into the trash, filling up the disposable towel holder. She sprayed disinfectant on all the surfaces and wiped them dry.

Going outside to feed her rabbits, Mandy thought again about Mark Boston. She wished she had asked his uncle where she might have seen him before. It had been bothering her all afternoon. Maybe in the morning she would remember.

But when Mandy awoke the next day she *still* couldn't think where she'd seen Mark before. She lay in bed, staring at the animal posters on the wall. Then she suddenly remembered all the work that had to be done to organize the show. She leaped out of bed, had a quick shower, and dressed in her usual jeans, sneakers, and sweatshirt.

She had just finished breakfast when Dr. Adam came in to ask Mandy if she'd like to help him take Sheba home. "Then I've just got time to take you to the sanctuary to see your owl before I do my rounds," he said.

"Thanks, Dad!" Mandy quickly ran the tap over her empty cereal bowl and left it to drain. She dashed out after him.

In the recovery room, Sheba stood on three wobbly legs, drinking a bowl of milk. She wagged her tail when Mandy appeared. Mandy felt relieved to see the dog looking better. Nevertheless, her heart still skipped with pity. No matter how hard she tried she could never get used to seeing animals in pain.

She bent down to stroke the dog's head. Sheba whined, then gave her a weak lick on the cheek.

"I've given her a painkiller," Dr. Adam said. "And I'll stop by and see her later to check her over."

"Can she walk?" Mandy asked.

Dr. Adam shook his head. "She'd probably try, she's a very brave animal. But we'd better carry her to the car, she's still pretty groggy."

Between them, Mandy and her dad carried the huge dog carefully out to the car. Dr. Adam had already laid a blanket in the back.

They settled Sheba down and Mandy climbed in with her.

"Good girl," she murmured comfortingly. "You'll be home soon."

Mandy stroked Sheba gently and whispered soft words of reassurance as Dr. Adam drove slowly along the street and up one of the narrow alleyways that led to Mr. Moon's house. It was called Moon Cottage and was one of a row of three stone houses with black tiled roofs and small, mullioned windows. There was a painting of a half-moon below the crescent-shaped door knocker.

Mr. Moon was looking anxiously out the window. He

disappeared as the car pulled up outside, then the front door opened and he came out and ran to the gate.

Mandy climbed out of the back as Dr. Adam came to lift Sheba out.

The dog's tail wagged joyfully and she licked his face all over as Mr. Moon bent to stroke her. Mandy swallowed back tears. It was always great to see animals reunited with their owners.

Mr. Moon helped Dr. Adam carry the dog indoors.

"Put her on the sofa," he said, shouting above the sound of loud pop music coming from a radio upstairs.

They settled Sheba down on the red blanket that covered the sofa. Mr. Moon closed a door so they could hear themselves speak.

"She still looks a little dazed," he said anxiously. He sat down next to Sheba and stroked her ears.

"Yes," said Dr. Adam. "She'll be groggy for a while." He handed Mr. Moon a bottle of pills. "Give her one of these three times a day," he said. "They'll control her pain. I'll stop by later to see how she's doing."

"Thank you so much," said Mr. Moon. "I'm very grateful for what you have done."

Mandy looked around the room. The walls were covered with Mr. Moon's watercolors. There was one of Stony Bridge and another of Monkton Woods knee-deep in bluebells like a wonderful azure carpet. It was so lifelike Mandy could almost smell their perfume.

"Do you like my pictures?" Mr. Moon asked when he saw Mandy gazing at them.

"Yes, they're lovely," Mandy said enthusiastically. "My friend James is good at art. I'm hopeless."

"Well, you have other talents," Mr. Moon said, his eyes twinkling at her. "We all have different things we can do well. Perhaps you would like to see my studio?"

"I'd love to," said Mandy.

"If you want to see that owl of yours I'm afraid we'll have to get going," Dr. Adam said, looking at his watch.

Mandy shrugged. "Sorry, Mr. Moon. I'll come back another time if that's OK."

"Any time you're in the neighborhood," Mr. Moon assured her. He saw them out.

Halfway along the village street Mandy let out an exclamation of dismay.

"What's up?" her father asked.

"I meant to ask Mr. Moon about Mark," she said.

"What about Mark?"

"Well, I know I've seen him somewhere before and I can't think where. I thought maybe his uncle might know."

"You'll have to ask him next time you see him," Dr. Adam said.

It was a beautiful, warm spring day as they drove the few miles to the sanctuary. When they got there, Dr. Adam stopped by the gate and honked the car horn. Betty came running out.

"We came to see the owl," Mandy explained as Betty unlocked the gate to let them through.

"He's still in the office," said Betty, nodding to Dr. Adam. "Come on in, both of you."

The owl was sitting on the perch in his hospital cage. Mandy approached cautiously. She didn't want to frighten him. His plumage looked less ruffled than before. His broad, speckled wings were folded against his tiny body. His large feet were spread out to help him balance on the narrow perch. He looked so sweet and funny, Mandy couldn't help smiling.

"He looks better," Mandy said, turning to the others with shining eyes.

"Yes," said Betty. "I've managed to persuade him to eat some earthworms and he's perked up a little. I'm going to put him into a flight cage later."

"What's that?" Mandy asked.

"It's a much bigger pen, outdoors," Betty explained. "The kind he'll be in over at the rehabilitation center. It'll give him a chance to get used to being out in the open. So far his only experience in the outside world was his fall from the tree!"

"Poor little thing," Mandy said softly.

"He needs room to stretch," said Dr. Adam. "And try to use his wings."

"That's right," said Betty. "If he doesn't he'll become very weak. He needs all his strength to learn to fly."

"How will you get him to do that?" asked Mandy.

"They'll do it over at Longmoor," Betty said. "I won't keep him here much longer. He's getting too used to humans and that's not good."

Mandy's heart went out to the little creature. It was true he looked better, more perky. But he still looked lost and lonely, and she felt desperately sorry for him, especially because it was her own fault the owl was there. Owls should be out in the woods and fields, flying free, not hunched up in a cage in someone's office.

She let out a sigh and turned away. "The sooner he's free, the better," she said.

Betty put an arm around Mandy's shoulder. "Mandy, don't feel so bad. If it wasn't for you, he might be dead by now."

"That's true," Mandy said. But she still wasn't certain she'd done the right thing.

"Tell Betty quickly about the show, then we've got to go," Dr. Adam told her.

Betty looked overjoyed when she heard how things were going. "Thanks, Mandy," she said giving her a hug. "I was wondering if you'd like me to bring my display of the work I do here. I've got photographs and information about stray dogs and cats, that kind of thing."

"That would be super," Mandy said. "Then people can see what will be done with the money we raise."

"And let me know if I can be of any help," said Betty.

"They seem to be getting on pretty well on their own," Dr. Adam said with a twinkle in his eye. "You know what Mandy's like once she gets started on something!"

"We're going to need lots of help on the day of the show," said Mandy. "So I'll let you know, OK?"

"Fine," said Betty. "I'll see you both soon." She stood by the gate as Mandy and Dr. Adam drove away.

Driving through the village Mandy spied James heading toward Animal Ark with a bundle of paper under his arm.

Dr. Adam stopped the car to let Mandy out and she ran over to meet him. Dr. Adam waved good-bye to his daughter and drove off.

Mandy told James about her visit to see the owl. James unrolled one of the fliers to show her.

"Wow, James, it's fantastic!" exclaimed Mandy.

Save **O**ur **S**anctuary!

WELFORD ANIMAL SANCTUARY

DESPERATELY NEEDS YOUR HELP

COME TO THE

GRAND NOVELTY VILLAGE PET SHOW

TO BE HELD IN

THE VICARAGE GARDEN ON SATURDAY

by kind permission of the Reverend Hadcroft

CLASSES FOR ALL PETS, BIG AND SMALL

THE FUN BEGINS AT 2 PM

"My dad helped," said James. "Then he went to his office to make all these photocopies."

Mandy was so pleased she felt like giving James a hug. Then she decided not to. She didn't want to embarrass him. James always blushed furiously whenever anyone gave him a hug.

"Come on," she said instead. "Let's take them around the village."

"What? You mean put one under everyone's door?" James said, looking dubious. "It'll take ages and we've got lots of other things to do."

Mandy looked crestfallen. "Well, who else is going to do it?"

James looked thoughtful. "I don't know."

Across the road, Clare McKay, the doctor's daughter, was coming out of the post office. She waved to Mandy and James and came across to talk to them.

"Hi," she said cheerfully. She held up her weekly animal magazine. "I just went to pick this up. The paperboy forgot to deliver it this morning."

Clare had been shy and hardly talked to anyone when she first moved to the house next door to James. But she adored animals and James and Mandy soon made friends with her. Together, they had managed to set up a refuge for a family of hedgehogs Clare had found living in her garden.

"What are you two up to?" The little girl stared at the bundle of fliers under James's arm.

Mandy told her and unrolled one so she could have a look.

"Wow, that sounds fun!" Clare said excitedly. "May I bring Guy and Sooty?" Guy was a blind hedgehog Clare looked after and Sooty was Clare's pretty pet rabbit.

"Of course," said Mandy. "And tell all your friends about it. We want as many people as possible, and animals, of course. We need to raise five hundred pounds at the least."

Clare's eyes widened. "Five hundred pounds!"

"Yep," said James. "So we need all the entries we can get. It doesn't matter what it is — pig or parrot, we'll have a competition for it."

Clare giggled and skipped away. "I'll tell Mom and Dad," she called. "They've got lots of friends with pets. They can all come."

When Clare had gone, Mandy looked thoughtful. They still hadn't solved the problem of getting the fliers out. Then, suddenly, she knew just what to do. She pulled at James's sleeve. "Come on. I've just had the most brilliant idea!"

Before James had time to ask what it was, Mandy dragged him rapidly off in the direction of the post office.

Seven

The post office doorbell clanged loudly as Mandy and James hurtled through the door.

"Yes, my dears," said Mrs. McFarlane, the post-mistress, as they dashed in. As well as being the village post office, the building served as the McFarlanes' general store. The shop sold all kinds of things like groceries, birthday cards, needles, and cotton. In fact, if you couldn't see what you wanted on the shelves, either Mr. or Mrs. McFarlane would go into the back, rummage around, and more often than not come up with what you wanted.

Mandy thought the shop was a little like Aladdin's

cave — full of hidden treasures. Best of all, there were jars full of old-fashioned sweets like mint candy, butterscotch, licorice balls, and delicious tangy lemon drops. The shop also sold the daily papers, and that was what had given Mandy her brilliant idea.

"What can I do for you this fine and sunny day?" Mrs. McFarlane was saying. "A quarter pound of lemon drops, perhaps?"

Mrs. McFarlane always had a smile for Mandy. She and her husband had known her since she was a toddler and were very fond of her. Mrs. McFarlane wore her graying hair drawn back in a bun and always had on a blue gingham smock. In fact, Mandy often wondered if she had any other clothes at all. She had spied Mrs. McFarlane in Walton market once and she *still* had that blue smock on!

"No, no sweets today, thanks, Mrs. McFarlane," Mandy said hastily. "We want to ask you a favor, don't we, James?"

"Er . . . yes," said James, although Mandy hadn't yet told him what her idea was.

Mandy took one of the fliers and unrolled it for Mrs. McFarlane.

". . . and you see," she said after explaining about the show, "I wondered if you would put one of these into everyone's newspaper."

At first Mrs. McFarlane looked a bit dubious but then she brightened up. "A pet show, eh? That sounds fun. Well, Mandy, I'd say yes straightaway, but Mr. McFarlane's gone up to Scotland to visit our daughter. I'm on my own in the shop this week."

"Oh," said Mandy, feeling disappointed. "Does that mean you won't be able to?"

"Not really," Mrs. McFarlane said. "But you'd have to come and put them inside the papers yourself. You see, I have to label them all with people's names and addresses so the paperboys and girls know where to deliver them. That takes a long time."

Mandy turned to James. "We can come and put them in ourselves, can't we, James."

"No problem," said James.

"The only snag is . . ." Mrs. McFarlane hesitated.

"What?" said Mandy. "We'll come and do it, honestly we will. It doesn't matter how early in the morning."

"Five o'clock?" said Mrs. McFarlane.

"Oh, you mean the day before," James said innocently.

Mandy nudged him. "No, silly. Mrs. McFarlane means five o'clock in the morning. Don't you, Mrs. McFarlane?"

Mrs. McFarlane smiled at James. "Mandy's right, I'm

afraid, James. The papers come at five and they have to
be all labeled and ready for the boys and girls at six."

James gulped. "Oh," he said in a funny voice. "Five
o'clock in the morning. Er . . . yes, that's fine, Mrs. Mc-
Farlane."

"Yes," said Mandy. "Absolutely fine." She sounded
confident, but deep down she was not quite sure how
she was going to get up that early herself. But it was no
good worrying. There was a job to be done and they'd
better do it.

Mrs. McFarlane held out her hand. "You leave those
with me then and I'll see you in the morning."

James gave Mrs. McFarlane the fliers.

"We'll keep one to give to Grandma," Mandy said,
pulling one from the bundle. "She belongs to a club in
Walton and I'm sure she'll put it up on the bulletin
board." She dragged James toward the door before he
changed his mind about showing up so early in the
morning. "Thanks."

Outside James looked upset. "How am I ever going to
get up at *that* time of the morning?"

"Set your alarm, silly."

James raised his eyebrows. "I know *that*, but what's
my mom going to say?"

"She won't mind. She knows it's for a good cause."

"I hope you're right," James muttered.

"Of course I'm right," Mandy insisted. "Now we've got to ask Jean about that tent!"

Back at Animal Ark, Jean Knox was studying the appointment book. She looked up as Mandy and James burst through the door.

"Simon said you know the lady who runs the scouts," Mandy said. "Could you ask her if we could borrow their tent for the pet show, please?"

"Pet show?" Jean frowned. "What pet show?" She took off her glasses and let them dangle on the chain around her neck.

"We're having a pet show to raise funds for Betty's sanctuary," Mandy explained patiently. "And we need a tent in case it rains. Please could you ask Mrs. Browne for us?"

Jean raised her eyebrows. "A pet show?"

Mandy was beginning to feel impatient. "Jean, will you ask Mrs. Browne for us or not?"

"Just as soon as I've got a minute," Jean said. "And if you two promise to keep out from under my feet today, I might even persuade her to let you have it for free." There was a twinkle in her eye.

"Oh, thanks, Jean!" Mandy's eyes shone. Everyone was being so kind. Mr. Hadcroft, Mrs. McFarlane, and now Jean Knox. Mandy had a feeling the Grand Novelty Village Pet Show was going to be a terrific success!

"Prizes next," said James, studying the list when they got back outside.

Mandy's face fell. "Oh, yes. Prizes. Come on, let's see who we can ask."

The village street looked sleepy in the morning sunshine. One or two people were heading toward the post office but Mandy didn't know them well enough to ask them to donate prizes.

They sauntered along by the village green hoping someone they knew might suddenly appear.

"It does seem a little rude," James remarked.

"What does?"

"Well, just asking people to give prizes. Maybe it isn't a good idea after all."

"What should we do, then?" Mandy said dejectedly.

But James had no ideas, either. He ran his hand through his hair. "I honestly don't know," he said, looking downhearted.

But Mandy refused to be beaten. "Let's take a flier to my grandma," she said. "She might have some suggestions."

James hurried to keep up with her.

Across the green they could see a familiar figure heading toward the Fox and Goose. It was Mark

Boston. They swerved across the green and ran to greet him.

"Hi, you two," he said, grinning broadly. "Thanks for bringing Sheba back with your dad this morning, Mandy. Sorry I missed you."

"Is she OK?" Mandy asked anxiously.

"A little groggy but she had a little walk around the garden. Or should I say a *limp* around the garden. Thanks again for your help yesterday, Mandy."

Mandy was just about to ask him why he looked familiar when someone called him from inside the pub. He waved his hand. "See you two later," he called, disappearing inside.

Mandy bit her lip. It really was bugging her. Next time she saw Mark she really would find out.

"Come on, James," she said. "Let's find Grandma."

They made their way over to Lilac Cottage. The sweet smell of the lilac tree wafted toward them as they went up the front path.

Indoors, Grandma was sitting at the kitchen table surrounded by guidebooks and maps.

"Where's Grandpa?" Mandy asked when she'd given her grandmother a quick hug and kiss.

"Out on his bike somewhere," Grandma said. "He muttered something about biking into Walton to get some greenfly spray. His bedding plants are being eaten alive."

Mandy sat down beside her grandmother and peered over her shoulder. "What are you doing, Grandma?"

"Planning our vacation," said her grandmother.

"Oh, Grandma, you're not going away?" Mandy said in a horrified voice. "Not before the show!"

Her grandmother patted Mandy's hand reassuringly. "Not until summer, darling. We're doing a tour of Scotland in the camper and I'm just planning the route."

"But Grandma, that's not for ages."

"Nonsense," said Grandma. "It'll come around in no time and I like to be organized, you know that."

Mandy grinned. That was typical of her grandma. She'd been known to organize her spring cleaning before Christmas had even come and gone. "Oh, Grandma, I'm glad you're not going away, yet. We need some more help with planning the show."

Grandma closed her notebook and gathered up the books and maps. "As a matter of fact, I've been having some thoughts on that, too. I've decided I'll run a cake stand."

"That's a great idea!" James exclaimed. Grandma's delicious cakes were sure to raise a lot of money.

"And your grandpa's decided to dig out that old feed

box out of the loft and we'll have a grab bag. Think that's a good idea?"

"Grandma, it's brilliant! What would we do without you?" Mandy gave her another hug.

"I've no idea." Grandma winked at James over the top of Mandy's shoulder.

James unrolled his flier. "Could you put this up in your club in Walton?" he asked. "Mandy said you probably would."

Grandma admired James's handiwork. "Did you do it, James?"

"Well," James went red, "my dad helped some."

"It's excellent. Yes, of course I'll put it up at our club. We've got a meeting tomorrow. I'll take it along with me."

"Thanks," said James.

"And we wanted to ask you about prizes," Mandy said. "Any idea where we could get some?"

"I could make a special cake," Grandma suggested.

"That's a good idea, Grandma," said Mandy. "But you'll be so busy baking cakes for the stand you might not have the time. We've only got until Saturday."

"That's true," said her grandmother. "If I come up with any bright ideas, I'll let you know. Meanwhile you could ask in the village shops. They might like to donate something."

"Now that *is* a good idea," Mandy got up from the table. "I knew I could rely on you, Grandma."

They left Mandy's grandmother to finish planning her trip to Scotland and wandered along the street. At the end of the path that led to the cottages behind the Fox and Goose they saw Grandpa's friend Walter Pickard, sitting in his front garden. One of his cats, Missie, lay asleep on his knees. The other two, Scraps and Tom, were curled up beside his chair.

"Hey, let's go and tell Walter about the show and ask him if he'll donate a prize."

They ran up the path and told him their news.

"That sounds like fun," Walter said. "I might even enter my three beauties." He stroked the ginger cat purring on his knee. Mr. Pickard adored his three cats.

"The trouble is," Mandy said with a frown, "we need some prizes. I don't suppose you can think of anything, can you, Mr. Pickard?"

Walter stroked his chin with his broad, callused fingers. You needed broad, strong hands to pull on the church-bell ropes. "Young miss, you could have a bunch of my champion roses," he said, tipping his old cap to the back of his head.

Mandy could smell their sweet scent wafting up from the rose bed beside the cottage.

"Oh, thanks," said Mandy. "That would be lovely, Mr.

Pickard." Walter Pickard's beautiful cabbage roses would make a great prize for a grown-up, but Mandy couldn't see a child being very pleased with them. But she wouldn't have hurt Mr. Pickard's feelings for the world.

Walter sucked thoughtfully on his pipe. Then he took it out of his mouth and popped it, still smoldering, into the top pocket of his old gardening jacket. "And I *might* be able to come up with something else," he added mysteriously. "Just leave it to me. I'll see what I can do."

Mandy gave a sigh of relief. Walter wouldn't let them down. It looked as if everything was falling into place at last.

They said good-bye to Mr. Pickard and wandered back toward Animal Ark.

Coming the other way was Ernie Bell. Ernie was a gruff old man, but he loved animals, and that made him all right in Mandy's book. He was the only person she and James knew who had a pet squirrel. He kept him in a huge run that he had built in his back garden. Mandy and James often took Sammy tidbits and loved watching the little creature's acrobatics. They *had* to tell Mr. Bell about the show. Sammy would make a perfect entrant for the most unusual pet category.

"I hope Mr. Bell's in a good mood," said James as they hurried across the road to meet him.

"So do I." Mandy made a face. Mr. Bell could sometimes be very grumpy although Mandy knew that under the harsh exterior there was a gentle heart.

"Hi, Mr. Bell," Mandy called cheerily as they ran over. She had learned long ago that the best way to deal with Ernie Bell was to give him her brightest smile and ask about Sammy the squirrel and Twinkie, his cat.

Ernie peered at them from under bushy eyebrows.

"How's Twinkie?" Mandy said, ". . . and Sammy? I haven't seen either of them for ages."

"They're fine," said Ernie, looking from one to the other.

"Have you heard we're having a pet show to raise money for the animal sanctuary?" said Mandy.

Mr. Bell frowned. "A pet show? What kind of a pet show? Not like that Crufts affair where people dress up their animals like dog's dinners."

Mandy giggled. "No, not at all. This is for all kinds of pets, not just dogs."

"Sounds like a lot of nonsense to me," said Ernie. "Why can't you just go around knocking on doors and asking for money? Plenty of other people do."

"Because we want people to have fun, too," Mandy explained. Ernie Bell was always grumbling about something — the weather, the cost of living — but he didn't really mean any of it.

"Hrrumph," said Ernie. "What exactly does Betty Hilder need the money for anyway?"

"Mostly repairs to the buildings," Mandy said. "Some of them are almost falling down."

"Hrrumph," Ernie said again. "She hasn't asked me."

"Asked you what?" said Mandy.

"If I could repair them," he said gruffly. Ernie Bell had been a fine carpenter in his day and still did some woodwork from time to time.

"Oh!" said Mandy, taken aback. "Would you?"

"I might," said Mr. Bell. He drew himself up to his full height. "If she asked me I might. I'm not past doing a few repairs, you know. I'm a fine carpenter. Best in the county."

"Oh, yes, I know," Mandy said hastily. "I could ask Betty if you like."

Mr. Bell shook his head. "No, thank you. I'll discuss it with her myself. When did you say this show of yours is?"

"Saturday," said James.

"Hrrumph," said Ernie. "Don't you go interfering, you two!"

"No, Mr. Bell," Mandy said meekly.

When the old man had gone, Mandy jumped for joy. "I bet it wouldn't cost five hundred pounds if Ernie Bell did it," she said.

"He might even do it for nothing," James said. "Then Betty could use the extra money for animal food or something."

A broad grin spread across Mandy's face. "James, I've got a feeling we might be helping Betty in more ways than one. Come on, I'll race you to the butcher's shop. We can ask Mr. Oliver if he'd like to donate a prize."

She sped away across the green. James was hot on her heels.

Mr. Oliver was just closing for lunch. Mandy averted her eyes from the bloodstains on his apron. She never ate meat if she could help it. But she knew lots of people did and a prize of a joint of beef might be just the thing.

"I'd be glad to, Mandy," said Mr. Oliver when he heard her request. "Betty does such a good job at that sanctuary. It would be a shame if it had to close."

James and Mandy crossed the green toward Animal Ark. Mandy's heart was singing. It had been a great morning. All they needed now were more prizes, the tent, a few more people to lend a hand on the day. The task of organizing the show was almost done. But, of course, the most difficult thing remained. They had to find someone important to present the prizes.

Back at Animal Ark, Jean Knox was shutting up shop for lunch. Dr. Emily had gone into Sheffield to the veterinary suppliers and Dr. Adam was still out on his calls. Mandy helped Jean carry her shopping bag to the car.

"I called Mrs. Browne," Jean told Mandy. "You can have the tent for nothing."

Mandy hugged her impulsively, almost squashing her glasses that still hung around her neck. "Thanks, Jean. We've had a terrific morning. Everyone's been really kind. Mrs. McFarlane's letting us put fliers in all the papers, Walter Pickard's lining up some prizes, and Ernie Bell might even repair Betty's buildings for her!"

Just then a magpie flew down, squawking, from the

tree in the Hopes' front garden. Jean gave an exclamation of dismay. She flapped her hands about.

"Shoo, shoo."

The bird gave another harsh squawk and flew off in the direction of the church. Then it circled and came back. It landed on the roof of Animal Ark and sat looking down at them like a king in his castle.

"That's bad luck, you know," said Jean, slamming the trunk of her car.

"Why?" asked James.

"There's an old saying about magpies. One for sorrow, two for joy."

Mandy made a face. She loved magpies with their beautiful greeny-black and white feathers and their long tails. "I don't believe any silly old saying," she declared. "I think magpies are beautiful."

Jean got into her car. "Mark my words," she said grimly through the open window. "Seeing a magpie brings bad luck."

They watched her drive away.

"Sounds like a lot of nonsense to me," said Mandy, imitating Ernie Bell's gruff voice.

But James didn't think it was funny at all. "I hope she's wrong," he said gloomily. "If this show's going to get off the ground, we're going to need all the *good* luck we can get."

"It's going to be great, James. Don't you worry about any silly old saying," Mandy said confidently.

James brightened up. "OK," he said with a grin. "I'd better go. I've got to give Blackie a bath. He rolled in something smelly this morning when I was taking him for a walk. Mom's tied him up in the garden and won't let him in until he's had a bath."

"Trust Blackie," Mandy said. "Don't forget to set your alarm in the morning!" she shouted as James set off for home.

"I won't!" he called back cheerfully.

But Mandy wasn't sure if James would be quite as cheerful at five o'clock the next morning!

Eight

Before evening office hours at the clinic, Mandy phoned Mr. Hadcroft to tell him about the arrangements they'd made so far.

"It all sounds wonderful, Mandy," said the vicar. "Let's hope the weather's good."

"We've lined up a tent," said Mandy. "The scouts are letting us have theirs for nothing."

As Mandy put the phone down, Dr. Emily came into the hallway.

"I've got to go to Twyford Farm to see a sick calf, then stop by the sanctuary with some eardrops for Betty's cats. Do you want to come?" she asked.

"I've been there once already today," said Mandy. "But I'd love to go again. Betty was hoping to put the owl in a flight cage and I'd really like to see him."

"Good," Dr. Emily said briskly. "Get your coat. It looks like rain."

"What's wrong with the calf?" Mandy called, dragging her coat off the peg in the hall.

Dr. Emily was getting her bag. "I can't be sure until we get there," she called. "Tom Hapwell just said it seemed very weak."

They drove quickly through the village, over the bridge, and took the narrow road up toward Twyford Hill. Across the valley ominous black clouds gathered. A dark curtain of rain seemed to be hanging from the sky in the distance.

Mandy peered anxiously through the windshield. "I hope it clears up by Saturday."

"Jean tells me you have a tent," said Dr. Emily.

"Yes," said Mandy. "But we want to set up parade rings outside if we can." She glanced at her mother. "It's going to be great, Mom. I'm really getting excited."

Her mother smiled and patted Mandy's knee. "Betty will be so pleased if you manage to raise lots of money."

"Yes," said Mandy.

"I've got a piece of good news for her anyway," said Dr. Emily.

Mandy's eyebrows shot up. Betty certainly could use some good news. "What?" she asked.

"I've found a home for the Shetland pony," said Dr. Emily.

"That's great, Mom!" Mandy's eyes shone. "Where?"

"One of the women in my yoga class," her mother explained. "I met her in the village and she wants a Shetland for her little girl."

Mandy couldn't wait to tell Betty.

As they approached Twyford Farm, Mandy chatted on excitedly about the show, only stopping when the car bounced over the cattle grid and into the farmyard.

A young man was mucking out the barn with a tractor and loader. He stopped the engine and jumped down from the cab. He wore green overalls and a black woolly cap. It was Mike Hapwell, the farmer's son.

"Hi, Emily. Hi, Mandy. Sorry to drag you all the way up here but I'm really worried. She's the calf of one of Dad's prize milkers. He and Mom are away on vacation and I'll really be in for it if they get back and find she's died."

"OK, let's take a look at her," Dr. Emily said in her usual businesslike manner. She took her bag from the car and headed toward the cattle shed.

"No, she's in the house," Mike said quickly. "I put her by the stove to keep warm."

In the farmhouse kitchen, a thin, newborn calf lay in front of the stove in a huge cardboard box.

Mandy's heart did a somersault. The calf really was doing poorly. She was thin and shivering and looked half-dead already. Mike had covered her with a blanket and she lay with her head resting on the edge of the box.

Mandy bent down beside the calf. Her eyes were dull and lifeless. Mandy had the horrible feeling their visit might have come too late.

"I found her in the corner of the barn," said Mike. "The mother had lost interest. Can you save her, Emily?"

Dr. Emily opened her bag quickly and took out a thermometer. She took the calf's temperature. By now, she was shaking violently. Dr. Emily held the thermometer up to the light.

"It's extremely high," she said, looking grim. She glanced up at Mike. "Don't look so worried," she said. "It's when the temperature's really low you have to start panicking. This means she's fighting some kind of infection. Get me a syringe please, Mandy."

Mandy took a syringe from its sterile wrapper and handed it to her mother.

"It's probably caused by the calf not sucking her mother's milk soon enough after birth," Dr. Emily explained. "That means she hasn't taken in any natural defenses." She quickly gave the calf an injection in her flank. "This is serum," said Dr. Emily. "It'll give her the necessary antibodies. Another one please, Mandy!"

Mandy handed her mother a second syringe. Dr. Emily gave the sick calf a second jab. "This is antibiotic to help fight the infection. You should see some improvement by later on tonight. If not, let us know. I'll come by again tomorrow."

Dr. Emily shut her bag and stood up.

"Thanks, Emily," said Mike.

Dr. Emily glanced at her watch. "Come along, Mandy. No time to waste."

Dr. Emily went outside to wash her hands under the yard tap. Mandy stayed behind, murmuring words of comfort to the sick animal. "Please get well," she whispered. She covered her up gently with the blanket, then hurried outside.

By the time she got to the car her mother had already started the engine.

They drove along the narrow hilly road to the sanctuary. The gate was closed and locked just as it had been earlier in the day. Mandy's heart gave a leap. By this time next week, she thought excitedly, it could be open again!

Betty came out to meet them and unlock the gate, and they drove through.

"Hello again, Mandy. I've put the owl in that flight cage around the back. Why don't you go and see him while I talk to your mom?"

"Thanks, Betty!" Mandy ran around to the back of the bungalow.

The tiny owl looked dwarfed in the huge flight cage. The cage was about nine feet high and twelve feet long. Inside, Betty had placed some logs and a branch of a tree that had come down in a high wind during the autumn. The owl was almost hidden as his speckled brown plumage mingled with the color of the wood. In fact, Mandy couldn't see him at all at first. It was only when he blinked his huge black eyes that she spied him sitting on the highest branch.

"Hello, Mr. Owl," she called gently, catching her breath. It was great to see him sitting up there, almost as if he were sitting in a branch of a tree in Monkton Woods.

On the ground below, Betty had placed two tiny dead chicks from the chicken farm.

Suddenly she heard Betty's voice behind her. "I'm hoping he'll come down and get them when he's hungry enough," she said. "He'll probably hop down at first but when I get him over to Longmoor, there'll be other owls and he'll learn to fly with them."

Mandy turned to her, eyes shining. "He looks much better, Betty. Thank you so much. He's obviously happier now that he's out of your office."

Betty put her arm across Mandy's shoulders. "I phoned the center today. They're looking forward to having him."

"When are you taking him?" Mandy asked.

"Probably early on Saturday morning."

Mandy would love to have gone with Betty but there were so many things to do for the show.

"I probably won't see him again then."

She peered into the cage. "Bye-bye, Mr. Owl." Her voice broke with a sudden feeling of sadness. "Good luck."

"Don't be sad, Mandy," Betty said. "It'll be great to know he's being looked after by experts."

Mandy nodded. "Yes," she said. She knew they were doing the right thing.

Just as they were saying good-bye, the phone rang.

Betty picked up the receiver. She began shaking her head. "No, I'm sorry, Mike, I can't."

The person at the other end said something else. Betty went on shaking her head. "I'm sorry, I just haven't got the funds."

Betty put the phone down. She turned to Mandy with

tears in her eyes. "That was P.C. Burton from Walton police station," she said. "Someone's brought in a dog that was abandoned on the highway."

Mandy gasped. "Oh, no! How could *anyone* do such a horrible thing?"

Betty shrugged. "It happens a lot," she said. "Tiny puppies often grow into great big dogs and people get fed up with them."

"But to abandon it out on the road," Mandy cried. "It could have been killed!"

Betty shrugged again. "I sometimes think that's what people intend," she said grimly. "Anyway, I told Mike Burton I couldn't take it in."

"Where will it go?" asked Mandy anxiously.

Betty shrugged. "He's going to try the SPCA."

Mandy stamped her foot. "If I met those people I'd put *them* out on the highway," she declared. "See how *they* like it."

Dr. Emily put her arm around her daughter's shoulders and gave her a hug. "Try not to take it to heart, Mandy."

"I can't help it," Mandy said furiously.

"Well, Mandy," Betty said. "If your show's a success maybe by next week I'll be able to take in stray dogs again."

"Oh, I hope so," said Mandy. "I really hope so!"

* * *

All the way home Mandy felt angry about the abandoned dog. At a quarter to five the next morning, she didn't feel much better. She hadn't slept very well. Plans for the show were whirling around in her mind. And when she did drift off to sleep she kept dreaming about magpies and calves and Mrs. Parker Smythe screaming at the sight of a mouse.

When her alarm went off Mandy jumped out of bed. She had warned her parents she would be getting up early. She dressed hurriedly. She went downstairs, grabbed a banana for breakfast, and crept out of the house.

The village looked tranquil and still in the early morning light. The sun was just rising, turning the rooftops a deep orange. *Red sky in the morning, sailor's warning*, thought Mandy. She hoped *that* saying wasn't any more true than the one about magpies. The shops and houses looked beautiful and peaceful in the clear, still morning light. It was almost as if the world had stopped turning and Welford was frozen in time.

Mandy suddenly stopped in her tracks. She drew in her breath and stood as still as a statue. Across the green, a large fox was rummaging about in the Dumpster outside the post office. Its head had disappeared inside. It emerged with something that looked like a half-eaten bun in its mouth. Mandy hardly dared breathe. The fox glanced around furtively, then sat on its haunches, chewing.

Mandy remembered a fox her dad had treated once up at the animal sanctuary. It had caught its leg in a snare. It would have died if it hadn't have been for Betty's sanctuary.

The fox's ears shot up as if it had heard a noise. Then, suddenly, it was gone, a red shadow disappearing up the road. It jumped a fence into someone's garden and disappeared.

Mandy saw the reason for the animal's sudden flight. James was plodding across the green, looking half asleep. His hair was tousled, his sweater on back to front. Mandy didn't want to tell him. He didn't look as if he was in a very good mood.

"Good morning," she said brightly.

James blinked behind his glasses. "Is it?" he grumbled.

"Cheer up," Mandy said, falling into step beside him. "You can go back to bed when you've done the papers."

James grunted.

Although it was only five o'clock, the post office was already a hive of activity. Mrs. McFarlane was sorting the newspapers into piles, writing house names and numbers on each one.

"Do you do this every day?" Mandy asked in disbelief.

The thought of getting up at five o'clock *every* morning filled her with horror.

Mrs. McFarlane went on sorting the newspapers. "Yes," she said. "Every day except Sunday. Then the papers arrive later."

"What time do they come on Sundays?" James asked.

"Half past six," Mrs. McFarlane said cheerfully. "We get to sleep in that day!"

James wrinkled his nose and ran his hand through his hair. Getting up at half past six didn't sound like sleeping in to him!

"Here." Mrs. McFarlane fished out the bundle of fliers from under the counter. "I've labeled that pile over there."

Mandy and James began to place one flier inside each of the daily papers. By the time the paperboys and girls turned up, the task was finished. Mrs. McFarlane put a stack of papers into each of their delivery bags, and they set off down the street.

James sat down on Mrs. McFarlane's stool. He still looked bleary-eyed.

"There!" said Mandy. "That didn't take long, did it? Thanks, Mrs. McFarlane!"

"You're welcome," the postmistress said. She reached up and took a box of chocolates off one of the shelves. "I heard you need prizes for your competitions. Will this do?"

Mandy drew in her breath. "Wow! Thanks, Mrs. Mc-Farlane. That's really kind of you."

Mrs. McFarlane went with them to the door. "My husband will be home by Saturday so I'm going to take the afternoon off and come to your show. I'm bringing Billy. Will there be a class for him?"

Billy was Mrs. McFarlane's green budgie.

"Oh, yes," said Mandy. "There's a prize for the most talkative budgie."

Mrs. McFarlane laughed. "Oh, dear. I'm afraid he only says 'Pretty boy.' But he whistles like the kettle and imitates the sound of the doorbell!"

"Well, that will count as talking, I'm sure," said Mandy. "Please bring him along. We'd love to see him. Wouldn't we, James?"

But James had wandered off down the street.

Mandy hastily said good-bye to Mrs. McFarlane and ran to catch up to him.

"I'm going back to bed," James mumbled.

"OK," Mandy said with a grin. "See you later. Don't forget there's still tons of work to be done!"

James yawned again and went off groaning.

After breakfast, Jean Knox popped her head around the kitchen door. Mandy was washing the dishes.

"I saw Mrs. Browne last evening. They're taking the tent over to the vicarage on Friday," she said.

"Thanks," Mandy said gratefully. "I'll go and tell the vicar."

The clinic was full as Mandy went through. She stopped to talk to one of the elderly Spry twins, Miss Marjorie. She was sitting huddled up in one corner with Patch, her cat, in a basket beside her.

Marjorie lived with her twin sister, Joan, at The Riddings, a large gothic house with a long drive and wide, sweeping lawns. It had been Mandy who had persuaded them to adopt Patch when she was an unwanted kitten.

It was unusual to see Miss Marjorie at the clinic and Mandy felt a pang of concern.

"I hope Patch isn't sick." Mandy peered into the basket.

Miss Spry's face gave a birdlike twitch. "She's been fighting," she said in a hushed voice as if it was something to be ashamed of. "She's a real little spitfire, I'm afraid."

"I'm sure Dad will fix her up," Mandy reassured the old lady.

Mandy went on to tell Miss Marjorie about the show. "Please enter Patch," she said. "She's such a lovely little cat. I'm sure she'd win a prize."

Miss Marjorie looked shocked. "Oh, no," she muttered, shaking her head. "Kitty might catch something from the other pets!"

Mandy couldn't help smiling. "I'm sure she won't do that. Please come, Miss Spry. Everyone would love to see you."

Miss Marjorie looked surprised and pleased in spite of herself.

"Oh . . . I'll have to ask my sister." The twins *never* did anything without consulting each other.

Mandy left Animal Ark and ran over to the vicarage. As she passed the Old School House, Eileen Davy was just coming out with a shopping basket over her arm. Mrs. Davy was a violin teacher and gave lessons to children in the village and in nearby Walton. She closed the garden gate and smiled when she saw Mandy pass.

"Hello, Mandy! I got your flier in with my paper," she said. "How are the plans going?"

"Fine, thank you, Mrs. Davy," said Mandy. "Everything's almost set. We just need to organize the prizes and find someone famous to present them. You don't know anyone famous, do you?"

Mrs. Davy smiled and shook her head. "No, I'm sorry, I don't. You need someone *really* special to draw the crowds."

"I know," said Mandy. "But who?"

"Have you asked Mrs. Collins? She's just about our most well-known resident."

Mandy nodded and explained why Mrs. Collins couldn't come.

"How about Amelia Ponsonby?" suggested Mrs. Davy. "She thinks of herself as something of a celebrity."

Mandy made a face. "Oh, Mrs. Davy, we don't want to scare people off!"

Mrs. Davy laughed. "No, you're right. Having Amelia present the prizes could be a problem. To be honest, Mandy, I can't think of *anyone*."

"Never mind," Mandy said with a sigh. "Maybe we'll think of someone. Although we haven't got much time."

"Well," said Eileen, "if I do, I'll let you know."

"Thanks," Mandy said. It was great to know people were so eager to help.

"Would you like a dozen new-laid eggs from my hens to give as a prize?" Eileen asked.

Mandy's eyes were wide. "Oh, yes, please."

"I'll bring them along on Saturday morning."

Mandy watched Eileen bustle off down the street, her shopping basket over her arm. Mandy ran off toward the vicarage. All they needed now was for Walter Pickard to come up with some more prizes and someone to present them. Then everything would be perfect!

Nine

Mandy made her way to the back garden of the vicarage. Mr. Hadcroft was in his shed, mending a puncture in his bicycle tire. He looked pleased to see her.

Mandy told him all about the plans for the show.

"The only thing is," said Mandy, "we still need someone really special to open it."

The vicar ran his hand through his dark curls, then he shook his head. "The bishop *might* have done it," he said. "But it's pretty short notice."

Just then, James turned up with Blackie.

"Come in and have some tea and cookies," said Mr.

Hadcroft, "and we'll work out where we're going to put the tables and things."

In the tiny kitchen, with its old-fashioned gas stove and scrubbed table, Mr. Hadcroft's tabby cat, Jemima, was asleep on a chair by the window. She got up and stretched as they came through the door. Blackie liked cats. He went to sniff her. But Jemima wasn't very fond of Blackie! She arched her back, her fur standing on end. A low growl came from her throat. With a laugh, Mandy scooped up the cat in her arms.

"Blackie won't hurt you," she said reassuringly. "Shoo, Blackie," she said to the Labrador. "You're scaring Jemima."

James helped Mr. Hadcroft make a pot of tea while Mandy sat by the fireplace with Jemima on her lap. She stroked the cat's soft fur. Then her fingers felt something underneath, on Jemima's tummy. Mandy frowned. There was a large lump growing just below Jemima's ribcage. She felt a stab of fear and her heart turned over. Lumps could be very dangerous.

"Did you know Jemima's got a lump on her tummy?" she said to the vicar. Mandy tried not to sound too worried. She knew how much Mr. Hadcroft loved his little cat.

Mr. Hadcroft looked shocked. "No, I didn't. Do you think it's anything to worry about, Mandy?"

"I think Mom or Dad should take a look at her," Mandy said.

"Oh, dear," Mr. Hadcroft said, his face full of concern. "I can't take her today, I've got some people coming for confirmation classes. I don't suppose . . ."

Mandy knew what he was going to say.

"Of course I'll take her," she said. "Do you have a cat carrier?"

"Yes, under the stairs. I'll get it."

He went out and came back five minutes later with a huge, old-fashioned cat carrier.

"The previous vicar left it," he explained. "Will it be OK?"

The carrier looked big enough to carry a half-grown tiger, let alone a cat!

"What did he keep here?" said Mandy. "A lion?"

The vicar chuckled. "No, I think he had several cats and used to take them away on vacation with him. Can you manage it between you?"

"I'm sure we can," said Mandy.

When they had finished their snack they went back out into the garden.

"They can put the tent up here," said the vicar, standing in front of the bay windows.

". . . and tables here," said James. "My dad's got three wallpapering tables we can use. I've already asked him."

"Perfect," Mandy said.

"And you could mark out the parade rings here," the vicar said, indicating a broad strip of lawn. "I've discovered some stakes and rope in the shed. They'll be just the thing."

Before long, they'd decided exactly where everything would go.

"All we need now is people and their pets," said James.

"They'll come," said the vicar confidently. "Especially after that wonderful flier you sent out. How could they resist?"

Back indoors, Mandy put Jemima gently into the cat carrier. "I'll take good care of her," she said to Mr. Hadcroft.

"Yes, I'm sure you will," he called confidently. But when Mandy turned to wave good-bye, Mr. Hadcroft was standing at the gate with his head bowed. Mandy felt a rush of pity. A cat like Jemima was such a good companion and Mr. Hadcroft would be lonely without her.

But behind her confident words, Mandy was very worried. If Jemima had had the lump for a long time, it could be too late to treat her!

Back at Animal Ark, the magpie was sitting on the gate. It flew off as Mandy and James came up the road. It settled on a high branch in the chestnut tree and stared down at them.

Mandy waved her hand. "Hello," she called.

James looked at her as if she'd gone mad.

"Well," Mandy said, shrugging. "If by any chance it *does* mean bad luck, we'd better be nice to it, hadn't we?"

They went inside and Mandy settled Jemima carefully into one of the animal cages at the back of the clinic.

Simon was there getting ready for early afternoon patients. Mandy explained why she'd brought the vicar's cat.

"Let's hope it's nothing too serious," he said. He went to tickle Jemima under the chin.

When Dr. Emily came in, Mandy told her what was wrong. She and James watched while her mom examined the cat thoroughly. Mandy's heart turned over as she saw the frown on her mother's face.

"It's not an abscess," said Dr. Emily. "It's a tumor of some kind. I'll have to remove it and send it off to the laboratory in Sheffield. They'll be able to tell me if it's serious or not. I'll call Mr. Hadcroft to ask his permission and find out if she's had any food recently. I can't operate until twelve hours after she's eaten. Put Jemima back, please, Mandy."

Mandy picked up the cat, cradling her soft fur against her cheek. She felt close to tears. She stroked Jemima's soft coat and placed her gently in the cage. She went out to the office, where her mother was telephoning Mr. Hadcroft.

"Mom," she said bleakly when Dr. Emily put the phone down. "It doesn't mean Jemima's going to die, does it?"

Dr. Emily gazed at her daughter. "I'm sorry, Mandy. I really don't know until we've got the results of the biopsy."

Mandy felt tears come to her eyes. "Couldn't you give her some medicine?"

Dr. Emily shook her head. "Mandy, if Jemima has

cancer we'll try to treat her, of course. But maybe, in the long run, the kindest thing would be to put her down."

Mandy's heart sank. It seemed so cruel. Jemima was only a young cat and should have many happy years ahead of her.

"We couldn't let her suffer, now, could we?" said Dr. Emily. She put her arm around Mandy's shoulders.

Mandy shook her head. Her mother was right, of course. She fought back tears for a minute. Then she squared her shoulders and sniffed. "Sorry, Mom," she said. "I'm OK now." She heaved a big sigh. "Where's James? We've got work to do."

James was in the kitchen, sitting at the table with pen and paper.

"OK," he said. "We'd better write out a program of events for the show."

They had just finished scheduling the events when Dr. Adam came in.

"Oh, dear, Mandy," he said, putting the kettle on for a cup of tea. "I'm afraid the weather forecast is pretty bad for the weekend. Rain all day Saturday."

But Mandy refused to be downhearted.

"We'll just have to hold the whole thing in the tent," she said. "Anyway, the weather forecasters are often wrong."

"True," said Dr. Adam. He rubbed his beard. "Let's hope they arc this time."

That afternoon, several people stopped by Animal Ark with prizes for Mandy and James.

Mr. Oliver brought the joint of beef. And minutes later, the grocer arrived with a box of groceries. Then Ernie Bell turned up.

"Here!" He thrust a bundle of something into Mandy's hand when she answered the door.

"What is is?" she asked, taken aback.

"Rhubarb," said Ernie. "That woman at the post office told me you wanted prizes. Will that do?"

"It's great!" Mandy gulped. "Thank you."

"You're welcome." Ernie turned abruptly and strode off down the path.

"Thank you, Mr. Bell," Mandy called after him. Mandy felt very grateful but couldn't really imagine anyone being pleased with a bundle of rhubarb as a prize. Perhaps Grandpa could use it for his grab bag.

"Come on," she called to James and Blackie. "Let's take it over to Lilac Cottage."

On the way, they met Mark Boston. He was taking Sheba out for her first walk since her accident. This time he had her firmly on a leash, although poor Sheba, hobbling along on three legs, didn't look likely to run off anywhere.

"Hi, you two," Mark called. "What do you think of the old girl now?"

Mandy crouched down to stroke her. "She still looks a little down in the dumps."

"She'd win the prize for the bravest dog," James piped up.

Mark frowned. "What do you mean?"

They explained about the show.

"Didn't you get a flier in your paper this morning?" asked Mandy.

Mark shook his head. "We don't get a daily paper. My uncle says the news makes him feel depressed. What's it raising money for?"

Mandy quickly told him about Betty and the animal sanctuary.

Mark's eyes widened. "And it's got to close, you say? Wow, that's a real shame."

"It's more than that," Mandy said glumly. "It's a disaster!"

Mark shrugged his broad shoulders. "What can I do to help? Just say the word."

"I don't suppose you know anyone famous, do you?" Mandy asked. "We need someone to give out the prizes — someone that'll make *everyone* want to come to the pet show."

"Huh?" said Mark raising his eyebrows. "Someone famous?"

"Yes," James said enthusiastically. "You know, a film star or something."

"I might," said Mark, smiling mysteriously. "I'll let you know."

Just then a white mini-bus pulled up outside the vicarage. Half a dozen scouts got out and began to take out a huge canvas tent from the back. Suddenly they stopped unloading the tent and stared at Mandy and James. Mandy recognized a boy from her class at school and gave him a quick wave. To her surprise, he ignored her and just went on staring.

"I'll see you guys later," said Mark, setting off back in the direction of Moon Cottage. He seemed to be in an awful rush.

Mandy and James hurried along to Lilac Cottage with their bundle of rhubarb. Mandy hoped Ernie wouldn't mind them giving it to Grandpa for his grab bag.

A delicious smell of baking greeted them as they went in the back door. Grandma was there, up to her eyes in homemade cakes. Mandy could hear her grandfather talking to someone in the sitting room.

"Yummy!" Mandy said, eyeing the counter covered

with sponge cakes, cookies, and apple pies. She went to take a closer look.

"Hands off!" Grandma warned, smacking Mandy's fingers. "You can buy one with your allowance at the show if you want to."

Mandy laughed. "I will — I promise."

Blackie's nose was level with the tabletop. It was quivering. He licked his chops, then barked, looking up hopefully at Mandy's grandmother.

"And keep that dog away!" Grandma warned again. She shooed Blackie outside.

Grandpa and Walter Pickard came in from the front room. Walter had a small cardboard box under his arm.

"Ah," he said when he saw Mandy and James. "Just the people I wanted to see."

Mr. Pickard handed Mandy the box. What on earth was it? Not more rhubarb she hoped. But no, the box was too small and too heavy.

She gazed up at Walter with shining eyes. "What is it?" she asked excitedly.

"Open it and see, young miss," Walter said in a mysterious voice.

Mandy carefully pulled up one of the flaps. She gave a loud gasp of surprise. Inside were rosettes — red, blue, green, and yellow. She looked at Walter.

"They're lovely. Thanks, Mr. Pickard!"

"Look underneath," Walter said.

Mandy peeled back the rosettes. Underneath them lay something else. Two rows of sparkling medals. They had "Welford Pet Show" engraved on one side. Mandy picked one up and turned it over. The other side was engraved with the words "First Prize."

Mandy's hand flew to her mouth. She looked at Walter, her eyes wide with surprise. "Wow, thanks, Mr. Pickard. They're absolutely wonderful!" she exclaimed breathlessly. "Real medals! They're just great! Look, James!"

"Glad you like them, young miss," said Walter. "I thought they were just the thing."

"Where on earth did you get them?" asked Mandy.

Mr. Pickard explained. "My son runs a sports shop in Sheffield. He dropped them off last evening."

Mandy put the box down and ran to give him a hug. "Oh, thanks, Mr. Pickard. You're so kind!"

"Steve was pleased to donate them," Walter said. "He's keen on animals, too. He might even come to the show with his Great Dane. It's huge. Have you got a competition for the biggest dog?"

Mandy shook her head. "No, we haven't, but there'll be something for him to enter. Oh, I hope your son comes. Then I can thank him for these gorgeous medals."

"I'd better take Blackie home and feed him," James said after he had looked at the medals and rosettes. "I think these cakes are just about too much for him."

"Come on, James," said Walter Pickard. "I'll walk back with you and you can tell me all about this show of yours."

"Thanks again!" Mandy called as they left. She sat down at the table with a sigh.

"Everyone's being so wonderful," she said. She picked up one of Grandma's magazines and began idly looking through it. Suddenly, something caught her eye. She stared and stared.

"Hey, Grandma, look!"

There, on the page giving details of the latest hit records, was a picture of Mark Boston! He looked very different — blond hair combed in front of his eyes, a pink leather jacket, and tight jeans. But it was definitely him.

Underneath the picture the caption read, *Mark Sparke, leader of Blue Moon.*

"Of course!" Mandy exclaimed. "His latest single's on the charts. How stupid of me not to recognize him. No wonder those scouts were staring. *They* knew who he was!"

Grandma peered over her shoulder. "Who?" she said, peering at the photograph.

"Don't you see? It's Mark, Mr. Moon's nephew. I *knew* I'd seen him somewhere before! Mark Sparke's his stage name!"

She went on to tell her grandma about Sheba's accident.

"Well, I never," said Grandma. "You know, I like that band."

"Blue Moon," said Mandy. "He must have taken the name from his uncle. I can't believe someone as famous as that is staying in our village!"

"What luck," said Grandma, wiping a smear of flour from her nose.

"He wants to come and live here —" Mandy said. She broke off. "Oh, Grandma, wouldn't it be amazing if *he* presented the prizes at the show? I thought he looked sort of funny when I asked him if he knew anyone famous. He must have thought I was joking."

"Well," said Grandma matter-of-factly, "if you want him to do it, you'd better go and ask him."

Mandy leaped up. She would do *just* that!

Mandy ran out of the house and along the main street toward Moon Cottage. She knocked on the door and waited anxiously for it to open. If Mark agreed to come to the show it would be the last of their problems solved. Everyone would want to come and see him and the show would be a terrific success — better than they

ever dreamed of. She shuffled her feet. *Hurry up,
Mark,* she said to herself. *Oh, please hurry up!*

Suddenly the door opened and Mr. Moon stood there
in his painting smock. He held a paintbrush in one
hand, a rag in the other.

He looked surprised to see her. "Oh, Miss Hope. How
nice. Have you come to see my studio?"

"Um . . . no, actually I've come to see Mark. Is he in,
please?" Mandy said quickly.

Mr. Moon shook his head. "I'm so sorry, he's just gone
tearing off to Walton. He's always in such a hurry, that
boy. He leaves me feeling quite exhausted."

"Do you know when he'll be back?" Mandy asked, her
heart sinking.

"Sorry," said Mr. Moon. "He didn't say."

Mandy told him the reason for her visit.

Mr. Moon looked doubtful. "He's going back to London tomorrow. I'm sorry, Miss Hope."

Mandy couldn't hide her disappointment. "Thanks,
Mr. Moon."

Mandy began to walk away, head down. She felt so
disappointed, she could cry.

She heard Mr. Moon calling her name.

"Please wait a moment, Miss Hope. I've got something for you."

Mr. Moon came back with something under his arm.

"Here," he said. "I've been hearing about your pet show. Would you like to give this as one of the prizes?"

Mr. Moon thrust a picture into Mandy's hands. She looked at it and gave a whistle. "Mr. Moon! Are you sure?"

It was a painting of Sheba as a puppy. She was sitting on the patio beside a clay pot full of bright red geraniums. Mandy thought it was the best painting she had ever seen.

"Yes, yes, of course I'm sure," said Mr. Moon, scratching his scalp with the end of his paintbrush. "I got Sheba from an animal sanctuary and I'm only too pleased to help."

Mandy stuck out her hands for Mr. Moon to shake. "Thank you *so* much," she gasped. "We'll keep it for the biggest prize of all."

"I've actually got a better idea," said Mr. Moon, stroking his beard thoughtfully. "Why don't you raffle it? It would be a way to raise extra money."

"What a good idea!" Mandy exclaimed. Then her face fell. "We haven't got any raffle tickets."

"I'm sure Mrs. McFarlane will find you some," said Mr. Moon.

"Yes, I'll go and ask. Thanks again, Mr. Moon."

Mandy walked along to the post office with the painting tucked under her arm. She tried desperately not to be downhearted about Mark. They had some great prizes now, all the posters were out, the tent was up in the vicarage garden. Everything was ready.

Mr. Moon was right. Mrs. McFarlane *did* have a book of raffle tickets. Mandy bought them and hurried home.

Dr. Adam and Dr. Emily were both out so Mandy showed the painting to Jean Knox, then left it in the kitchen for her parents to see when they came in. She took the box of medals upstairs and put it on her windowsill. She opened the lid. She took out the medals one by one and laid them in a line along the windowsill. They were so shiny and beautiful, and she felt very lucky to have them. She was determined not to be upset about Mark. Everything else was going well. Still, it was disappointing that Mark would miss the show.

Through the open window, Mandy saw her father's Land Rover pull up outside. She rushed downstairs to show him the painting.

He came into the kitchen. "Wow!" he said when he saw it. "That's terrific. Where did you get it from?"

Mandy told him.

"That was kind of him. His pictures sell for a lot of money, I believe."

By the time Mandy and Dr. Adam had eaten their lunch and Mandy had done her chores in the clinic, half the afternoon had gone. There had been no word from

Mark so Mandy could only think he hadn't got her message. She went back into the kitchen. Mr. Moon's picture was still propped up against the fruit bowl. She decided to take it up to her room for safekeeping.

The box of rosettes was on the windowsill. Mandy suddenly remembered the medals. She had better put those away, too.

But, to Mandy's horror, the medals were nowhere to be seen. She was sure she had left them in a long, shiny row on her windowsill. Her heart lurched. Where had they gone?

She put the painting on the bed and hurriedly opened her dressing-table drawer. Maybe she had put them in there? Perhaps her mom had come in and decided to tidy up? But surely she and her dad would have heard her.

Mandy flew around the room in a panic. She opened all her drawers, her cupboards. She searched frantically in her desk. She stood in the center of the room, her hands in her hair. What had happened to those beautiful medals? Where on earth had they gone?

Mandy ran over to the open window. She looked out at the garden below. Had they fallen out?

She rushed downstairs. Out in the garden she searched high and low. Her dad came out to ask her what she was up to.

"The medals!" Mandy turned a stricken face toward him. "They've disappeared!"

They looked everywhere but they couldn't find a single medal.

"I don't understand," Mandy wailed. "I left them on the windowsill. I know I did!"

When Dr. Emily came in she searched as well. She took another look in Mandy's room. She peered under the bed, hunted in the cupboards. There was no sign of the medals anywhere.

"Now everything's ruined!" Mandy sobbed. "What will Walter Pickard think of me!"

"They still might turn up," said Dr. Emily, trying to comfort her daughter.

But whatever had happened to the medals was a complete mystery. They had disappeared into thin air!

That night, Mandy hardly slept a wink. The wind howled around the house and rain lashed against the windowpanes. Mandy turned her head into the pillow with a sob. Everything seemed to be going wrong. There was no one to present the medals and now no medals to present. Jean Knox had been right when she told Mandy about that magpie. It *had* brought bad luck after all!

Ten

It was the day of the Grand Novelty Village Pet Show. Mandy awoke early. She leaped out of bed and drew back the curtains. Her heart sank. Not only were the medals missing, the weather was terrible. Black clouds covered the sky and the rain was coming down in buckets.

Mandy took a deep breath. They'd just have to have the whole thing in the tent. After all, that's what it was for!

Mandy hurriedly dressed. Everyone knew about the show now. It had to go ahead, rain or shine.

Downstairs, Dr. Emily was setting the table for breakfast.

"Come on, Mandy. You've got a busy day ahead of you."

Mandy sat down, trying not to look miserable. She toyed with her bowl of cornflakes.

"Eat up!" Dr. Emily put a plate of eggs and toast in front of Mandy's father.

Dr. Adam looked up from his paper. "Cheer up, Mandy," he said. "Maybe it'll stop raining soon."

"It's not that," Mandy said, staring into her orange juice. "It's those beautiful medals. I wish I knew what had happened to them."

Dr. Emily put her arm around Mandy. "I'll have another look later," she promised. "Maybe they'll turn up."

"Thanks, Mom."

Suddenly, Dr. Adam gave a low whistle. "Hey, Mandy," he said. "Look at this!"

He turned the paper toward her. The headline said, *Pop star to present prizes at village pet show.*

Mandy could hardly believe her eyes. She gave a gasp and grabbed the paper from her dad's hands. She quickly read the story. "'Pop star Mark Sparke is lending his support to a grand pet show to raise funds for the Welford Animal Sanctuary . . .'" she read aloud. The story went on to give all the details of the show.

Mandy looked up with shining eyes. "Wow!" she said. "That must have been where Mark rushed off to yesterday. His uncle said he'd gone into Walton. He must have gone to the newspaper office." She beamed a smile at her mother and father. "Good old Mark!" Suddenly the loss of the medals didn't seem quite so tragic after all.

Mandy hurriedly gulped down her orange juice. She took a mouthful of cornflakes. "I'm going to go thank him," she called.

"But Mandy, finish your —" her mother began. But Mandy was gone, rushing down the street and along the lane to Moon Cottage.

Mark answered her knock at the door.

Mandy gave him a bright grin. "I've just seen the paper," she panted. "Thanks, Mark!"

Mark shrugged. "I'm glad to help," he said. "Is there anything else you'd like me to do?"

Suddenly Mandy had an idea. "You could take care of the raffle," she said. "Your uncle's given us a picture of Sheba. Everyone will buy a ticket if you're selling them." Mandy felt herself go red. Now that she knew Mark was a famous pop star, she felt a little shy.

"No problem," said Mark. "I'll be glad to."

"Oh, thanks," Mandy said breathlessly.

"What time does the fun start?" Mark called as Mandy ran down the path.

"Two o'clock," she called. "See you later!"

Skipping back along the road, Mandy realized it had

stopped raining. The black clouds were rolling away and the sun was coming out. Her heart gave a leap. Things just might work out!

Up in the chestnut tree, the magpie flew squawking from its untidy nest. It was joined by another one and the two birds flew around in circles before settling back in the tree.

"One for sorrow, two for joy," Mandy murmured to herself.

Mrs. Platt from the bungalows was walking along with her miniature poodle, Antonia. Antonia had been one of Betty's dogs from the sanctuary.

The poodle was looking splendid in a red collar, her coat clean and fluffy. She greeted Mandy with a lick and a wag of her tail.

"Are you bringing her to the show this afternoon?" Mandy asked as Antonia jumped up to say hello.

"I certainly am," Mrs. Platt said proudly. "I want to give my support to the sanctuary. I'd never have gotten Antonia if it wasn't for Betty Hilder."

"It's going to be a lot of fun," said Mandy, feeling excited. "Mark Sparke's presenting the prizes."

Mrs. Platt looked blank. "Mark who?"

"Mark Sparke, the pop star. Haven't you heard of him?"

Mrs. Platt shook her head. "No, sorry. But never

mind, I'm sure all the young people will know who he is." She looked up at the two magpies squawking overhead. "Nasty, noisy things, magpies," she said. "They're thieves, too."

"Thieves?" said Mandy, puzzled.

"Yes, they love to take shiny things and keep them in their nests. I once heard about . . ."

Mandy frowned. Thieves? Thieves! She suddenly gave a whoop of joy. She threw her arms around Mrs. Platt and gave her a hug. Of course! *That's* where the medals had gone. Mandy had left her window open and the magpies had stolen them!

Mandy sped away. "Thanks, Mrs. Platt," she called over her shoulder.

Mandy ran indoors. "Mom? Dad? Where are you?"

But the house was empty.

"They've both had to go out." Jean Knox had just arrived at the clinic and was hanging up her coat. "Sam Western's got some big emergency on his farm — they could be ages."

Mandy's mind raced. James's dad would have a ladder. She rushed over to James's house. He was just coming out, on his way over to Animal Ark.

"They've taken the tables over to the vicarage," he said as Mandy blurted out her story. "But Dad's ladder is in the shed." James dashed down the garden path and wrenched open the shed door. "Come on, let's do it ourselves!"

Together they carried the ladder across the green. Mandy set it firmly against the tree trunk.

"You hold it," she told James. "I'll climb up."

"Don't look down," James warned. He squinted upward.

Carefully, Mandy climbed all the way to the top. The two magpies watched her, their eyes bright against their shiny black heads. With one hand, Mandy held on tightly to a nearby branch. She leaned across. The ladder swayed.

"Be careful," James yelled from down below.

By now, a small crowd had gathered to watch.

Ernie Bell shook his head. "She shouldn't be up there," he said. "It don't look safe to me."

Then, as Mandy reached into the nest, her hand came into contact with something. Something round and cold. She picked it up. To her relief, it was one of the medals! She reached in again.

Soon all the medals were safe in Mandy's pocket. A small cheer went up as Mandy climbed carefully back down the ladder.

James patted her on the back. "Great job, Mandy!"

"Come on," Mandy said. "Let's get the rosettes and take everything over to the vicarage before they disappear again!"

They took the ladder back, then collected the rest of the prizes. They made their way over to the vicarage.

The garden looked clean and bright after the rain. The grass sparkled and the flowers looked shiny and fresh. Mr. and Mrs. Hunter had set the tables up along one side of the lawn. The vicar had already staked out the show rings.

They found Mr. Hadcroft in the tent talking to Mandy's grandmother. She was busy setting up her cake stand.

Then Mandy's grandpa arrived with his grab bag bin and a big cardboard box full of prizes. Walter Pickard was with him, carrying a huge bunch of his beautiful roses.

Soon, the whole vicarage garden was a hive of activity. People were bustling everywhere, setting up platforms, arranging prizes on the table.

Mrs. Browne stopped by with a megaphone. "I thought you might need this to announce the competitions," she told Mandy.

"Yes, thanks," Mandy said. Her face fell. "Who's going to do that?" she said to James.

"You can," James grinned. "I'm going to be busy getting the entries organized."

Betty turned up in her old station wagon. Mandy and James helped her unload her display boards. They set them up in the tent.

The morning flew past and soon it was one o'clock. Mandy looked around. Everything was ready. The tables, the parade rings, posts with arrows pointing to the parade rings and stands. On a table by the gate was a pile of entry forms for the various competitions. That was going to be James's job. He would take the money and write down the names of the entrants. Her heart began to pound. Only an hour to go. She couldn't wait!

Then Mandy suddenly realized she had not seen her parents all morning. Surely they couldn't *still* be at Sam Western's?

She dashed over to Animal Ark. Simon was just locking up as she arrived.

"Simon, where are Mom and Dad? They're supposed to be at the vicarage. The show starts at two and Mom and Dad are the judges."

"I know," said Simon. "I was just coming to tell you. They're still up at Upper Welford Hall with Mr. Western. I've got a horrible feeling they're not going to make it."

Mandy rushed back to the vicarage to tell everyone the bad news.

"That wretched man," Grandma said angrily. "I bet he's done it on purpose!"

"But what can we do?" Mandy said anxiously. "We can't have a pet show without any judges."

"*You'll* have to do it," said James. "You know lots about animals."

"I can't be the announcer and the judge," Mandy said desperately.

But Grandpa always looked on the bright side. "Well," he said matter-of-factly, "we'll just have to hope they get back in time, that's all."

When it was almost time for the show to begin Mandy sat down on a chair beside the tent. Mark had arrived and was talking to Betty. Grandma was standing by her cake stand waiting for her first customer, and Grandpa was checking his grab bag bin to make sure there were enough prizes. James and Mr. Hadcroft were waiting by one of the rings with Blackie. Mandy looked down at the pile of entry forms on the table beside her. Suddenly the church clock struck two. Surely people should be here by now. Maybe no one was coming after all!

Eleven

Just as Mandy was about to give up hope of anyone coming to the Grand Novelty Village Pet Show, there came the sound of a vehicle pulling up outside the vicarage. Mandy ran to the gate. A mini-bus was parked outside and people were piling out. Not only people, but pets of all kinds. There were dogs on leashes, cats in carriers, budgies in cages.

Mandy's grandma had come up behind her. "Oh, wonderful!" she cried, clapping her hands. "It's my friends from our club in Walton." She ran down the path to greet them.

Mandy saw something else. A string of people walking down the street and across the green toward the vicarage. She recognized lots of them: Mrs. McFarlane
with her budgie; Mrs. Williams with her cat, Walton; Susan Price leading her pony, Prince. There was little
Tommy Pickard, Walter's great-grandson, with his hamsters in a cage; Clare with her rabbit and hedgehog
coming along with Lydia and Houdini, her prize goat.
Behind them came Mrs. Markham with Bunty. Then
Mandy spied Ernie Bell with Twinkie in a carrier and
Sammy the squirrel leaping about in a cage.

Mandy's heart brimmed with happiness. There were
so many people! She could hardly believe her eyes. To
her surprise, Mrs. Ponsonby pulled up in her large car.
She climbed out and went to get both Toby and Pandora
from the special compartment at the back. Pandora
was groomed to perfection. She had a red bow in her
collar. Toby wore one the same color. And Mrs. Ponsonby wore a red hat to match. She swayed up the path
in a long skirt like a ship in full sail. Even Imogen
Parker Smythe turned up in her pink Lycra leggings and
white fluffy sweater. Her mother held her firmly by the
hand.

"Now, watch out for those rats," Mandy heard her say
as they went past.

"I want a rat!" Imogen was saying.

Mandy chuckled. If there was a competition for the most spoiled child, Imogen would definitely win!

Mandy felt full of rapture. It looked as if the whole village had turned up to support her cause. This was going to be an afternoon to remember!

She greeted people as they came through the gate. "James will give you your entry forms," she explained, ushering them through. She glanced anxiously over toward Animal Ark. There was still no sign of her mom or dad. James was right. If her parents didn't turn up in time, she would just have to do the judging herself!

But then she saw her dad's Land Rover heading toward the vicarage. It pulled up with a screech of brakes. Dr. Adam and Dr. Emily leaped out.

"Mandy," her mom gasped. "Sorry we're late. Sam Western kept us talking. He knew you were having the show today. I wouldn't be surprised if he hoped we'd be forced to miss it!"

"Never mind." Mandy grabbed their arms and dragged them up the garden path. "You're here now. I think everyone in the whole world has turned up!"

Mandy stepped up onto the platform and grabbed the megaphone.

"The competition for the dog with the waggiest tail is

just starting in Ring One," she announced. "Will all entrants please take their places."

About two dozen people and their dogs filed into the parade ring. Dr. Adam stood leaning his chin on his hand, watching them walk around. Mrs. Ponsonby had left Imogen Parker Smythe in charge of Pandora while she proudly marched along with Toby. As she spoke to him his tail wagged like mad.

"I bet Toby wins," Mandy said to Mark, who had come up by her side. In his hand he held an old ice cream carton filled with fifty-pence pieces. "The raffle's going great guns," he said.

Mandy turned with shining eyes. "Isn't it wonderful that so many people have come?"

"And it's all thanks to you and James," Mark said.

"And you," said Mandy, blushing.

The parade of dogs was still going on. Dr. Adam raised his hand. "That's fine, thank you. I've made my decision."

"Oops," said Mark. "I'd better do my stuff." Mandy handed him one of the medals from her shoulder bag. Mark strode into the ring and shook hands with the winner. Dr. Adam had chosen a small boy with a Welsh collie whose tail wagged so fast it was just a blur. There was a blue rosette and a dozen of Eileen Davy's free-range eggs for the runner-up.

In the tent, Dr. Emily was judging the most unusual pet. A row of people were lined up behind one of the wallpapering tables with cages and boxes of all varieties. There were so many to choose from — a child with a stick insect; a huge man in a leather jacket and motorbike boots with a huge, hairy tarantula; a woman with a pet hen; Ernie Bell with his squirrel, Sammy. In the end the prize went to James's friend with the pet wood louse.

"Her name's Valerie," the boy told Mark as he presented the winner's medal. Mark grinned and peered into the box. He confided to Mandy later that he couldn't even see poor Valerie!

Mandy was just waiting to announce the start of the rodent with the twitchiest whiskers competition when there was a shout from the tent. Suddenly Blackie appeared with something in his mouth. After him ran Grandma, waving her fist. Then came James, Blackie's collar and leash dangling uselessly from his hand.

"He's stolen a cupcake," James shouted, laughing.

Mandy collapsed into chuckles. She laughed louder when Grandma came back, dragging Blackie by the scruff of his neck. Blackie didn't look as if he cared one bit — *and* he was licking his chops furiously. By now, Grandma was laughing, too. She scolded Blackie, then gave in and hugged him. "You bad dog!" she said, her eyes shining with tears.

James had turned red. "Sorry."

Mandy's grandmother put her arm around him. "Never mind, James. I'll forgive him. One thing about Blackie — he's got good taste!"

Just then there was another cry from the corner of the garden. Mrs. Ponsonby was standing on one of the garden seats, her long skirt held up over her knees.

"A rat!" she screamed. "A rat! Vicar, Vicar, help me!" Poor Pandora was tucked under one arm, Toby under the other. Both dogs yelped and wriggled frantically as a sleek white rat ran around under the seat. Suddenly it shot out. Mrs. Ponsonby screamed so loudly her hat fell off — right on top of the rat!

A little girl ran out from the crowd and knelt down on the grass. She carefully raised the brim of Mrs. Ponsonby's hat. Two black eyes and a snuffling pink nose peeped back out at her. She picked up the rat and held it close to her face. "Naughty Gladys," she said and kissed its nose. She went off to one of the show tables, still scolding her pet.

When she was sure the rat was a safe distance away, Mrs. Ponsonby drew herself up to her full height and stepped regally off the chair. She put her dogs down.

They both ran off after the little girl. Mrs. Ponsonby bent to pick up her hat. She placed it on her head with a sniff and went off after her pets.

Then Mandy heard an argument going on behind the tent. It was Ernie Bell and Myra Hugill. Mrs. Hugill was chairman of the Welford Women's Club and wasn't used to being argued with.

"I tell you Twinkie is the prettiest cat in the village," Ernie was saying angrily. "And she's the best mouser."

Mrs. Hugill waved her umbrella at him. "Felix caught sixteen mice last summer. I'm sure Twinkie couldn't beat that."

"Oh, yes —" Ernie began.

But Mandy interrupted them. They sounded like two children on the school playground.

"Both your cats are adorable," she said, taking each one by the arm. "Now, come on, please don't argue. Everyone's supposed to be having a good time."

Mrs. Hugill looked sheepish. "Yes, sorry, Mandy."

Ernie Bell snorted and strode off toward the tent. "I'm going to talk to Betty Hilder," he said.

"He's just annoyed because Twinkie didn't win a prize," Mrs. Hugill said. Then she blushed. "Felix won second place and that nice pop singer presented him with a rosette and a joint of beef." She glanced over her shoulder. "He gave me a kiss," she whispered in Mandy's ear. "He's a very nice young man."

"Yes, he is." Mandy couldn't help grinning. It looked as if Mark was a big hit! People had been crowding around him all afternoon. Last time Mandy tried to count how many people had turned up, it seemed as if not only had all the village folk come but half of Walton as well!

Mandy went to find her mother. She was talking to Mr. Hadcroft.

"I phoned the lab this morning," she said. "There's no need to worry about that lump. Jemima's going to be fine."

The vicar looked relieved. "Thanks, Emily," he said gratefully. "I don't know what I'd have done if it was anything serious."

Mandy was just about to say how pleased she was to hear the good news when she felt someone tug at her sleeve. It was Betty. Her eyes were shining.

"Mandy, this is the best day of my life! I've just been talking to Ernie Bell and he's offered to repair the animal pens free of charge if I provide the materials."

Mandy smiled. "That's great, Betty. He's a really good carpenter. Do you remember that wonderful cage he made for Lucky the fox cub?"

"Yes, I do," Betty said. "And what's more, Mark has offered to adopt several of my animals. That means he's going to pay for their food and vet's bills."

"Oh, Betty, that's fantastic!" Mandy's heart was brimming with joy.

Betty gave her a hug. "Mandy, I'm so grateful to you."

The rest of the afternoon seemed to fly past. When all the competitions were finished, Mandy and James organized a grand cavalcade of animals.

The pets and their owners paraded into the ring. Susan Price led the way with her pony, Prince. Prince's coat shone. Then came Lydia with Houdini. Houdini was prancing about and being mischievous as usual. Clare came into the ring with Sooty the rabbit and Guy, her hedgehog, in a wooden box; Mrs. Ponsonby and Pandora and Imogen Parker Smythe holding Toby's leash trotted behind.

James was next, trying desperately to keep Blackie to heel. He wasn't having much luck. Blackie kept leaping forward trying to overtake everyone and lead the way. He was determined to be the first in something!

The Spry twins came next with Patch, then Walter Pickard with all three of his cats. There was Mrs. Platt and Antonia, followed by Grandma's friends from Walton with all kinds of dogs and cats. Someone had even brought their parrot in a tall wire cage. "Pretty Polly," it screamed. "I'm simply the best!" Everyone burst out laughing.

Mandy stood at the edge of the parade ring. She suddenly realized just how many of the people walking around were her friends. And their pets were her friends, too. She felt proud to know them. They had all turned out to support her and James in their bid to save the sanctuary.

Mandy sighed. What a fabulous afternoon it had been!

There was a round of applause as the competitors filed from the ring.

Betty had gone to stand on the platform and was making a short speech. Mark stood beside her, looking pleased with himself. He held a bucket full of folded-up raffle tickets.

"I want to thank everyone for their kindness," Betty said to the listening crowd.

Mr. Hadcroft came up to Mandy. He looked delighted. "Your grandpa and I have just counted the money. We've raised over six hundred pounds. Isn't that wonderful?"

"Six hundred pounds!" Mandy couldn't believe her ears. She had to tell Betty right away.

Mandy stepped up onto the platform and whispered

in Betty's ear. Betty's eyes widened with surprise and pleasure. "Mandy, that's wonderful!" She turned back to the crowd. "Mandy has just told me we've raised over six hundred pounds," she announced. "I just want to thank you all for your generosity. And most of all . . ." she said, beckoning to Mandy and James, ". . . I want to thank these two young people for all their hard work on behalf of my animals."

Mandy and James blushed as the crowd clapped and cheered.

"It just remains for Mr. Hadcroft to draw the winning raffle ticket," said Betty.

The spectators fell silent as Mr. Hadcroft put his hand in the bucket and drew out a ticket. He handed it to Mark.

Mark unfolded the ticket, then looked up with a grin. "Number sixty-four," he called. Then he looked on the back. "Mandy Hope," he said. He picked up his uncle's painting and handed it to her. "Well done, Mandy!"

Mandy gasped. How on earth could she have won the painting? She hadn't even had time to buy a ticket. She was just about to say as much when she heard her mother's voice behind her. "I bought you a ticket, Mandy," she explained, giving her a hug. "I'm so glad you've won — you really deserve it."

"Hear, hear," said Mark. To Mandy's embarrassment he bent and gave her a kiss on the cheek.

Mandy blushed. She stared at the picture, then at her mother. "Wow, Mom, thanks! I'll put it up in my room."

Mandy took a pound coin from a tin can with all the proceeds and handed it to the vicar.

"I haven't forgotten my promise," she said. "This is for the church roof."

Mr. Hadcroft took it from her. "Thank you, Mandy. If we're as successful as you've been today, we'll have a new roof in no time!"

As people began filing out, Betty took Mandy to one side.

"I took the owl over to Longmoor Rehabilitation Center early this morning, Mandy," she said. "I felt he had been with me long enough."

"Oh . . ." Mandy felt a pang of sadness.

"I saw Tom Tyrrel, the man who runs the place," said Betty. "He said they'll keep him for three to four months, then they'll be able to release him back into the wild."

"Where will they do that?" asked Mandy. She wanted to know where the owl would be and that he would be safe and happy and free.

"He'll be released in a place called Carter's Wood," Betty explained. "It's a site that they survey regularly.

They know there's plenty of prey there for owls, and plenty of trees for them to shelter and nest in. Tom said there's no need to worry about him. He'll be absolutely fine."

Mandy felt tears come to her eyes. She would love to have been there when the owl was released, but she knew that the less contact owls had with humans, the better.

James came up beside her and saw her looking sad. "What's up, Mandy?"

Mandy told him.

"Betty had to take the owl," said James. "He had to be in a proper place so they could get him ready to be released."

"Yes, I know," said Mandy. And although she had longed to see him just once again she knew James was right. In a few months, her owl would be free. Free to hunt over the fields and woodlands. Free to feel the air through his feathers and free to live life as nature intended. And after all, if it hadn't been for that pathetic little bundle Mandy had found on their walk in Monkton Woods, she might never have known that the sanctuary was under threat. At least now the tawny owl wouldn't be the very last creature that Betty would save.

The sun was going down as Mandy and her parents walked back across the green toward Animal Ark. The village was tranquil now. All the cars had gone and the shops were closed for the day. Outside the post office, a little black cat sat washing itself by the wall. The church clock chimed six. Mandy felt exhausted but very, very happy. She knew she would never forget the wonderful day that Welford saw its first Grand Novelty Pet Show. Would it become an annual event? After all, the sanctuary would always need funds. She sighed and linked arms with her mom and dad, matching her strides with theirs. Life was just grand!